The Fryeburg Chronicles: Book I

The Amazing Grace

By June O'Donal

The Fryeburg Chronicles: Book I
The Amazing Grace
by June O'Donal

Printed in the United States of America

ISBN 9781613796306

www.xulonpress.com

In Loving Memory

To My Father, Albert A. Amaral
Who shared his love for history with me.

Table of Contents

Acknowledgements

I am no Sarah Miller. I have the following people to thank for educating me in the many skills and crafts portrayed in this novel.

I wish to thank Erica Boynton at Remick Country Doctor Museum and Farm in Tamworth, New Hampshire (www.remickmuseum.org) for teaching me how to cook on a hearth, churn butter and make sausage. Most of the recipes and meals in this story are from her Hearthside Dinners.

The talented staff at Sturbridge Village in Sturbridge, Massachusetts demonstrated how to dip candles and make fur mittens. Time spent in the kitchen in a farm house and studying the contents of their spice box, touring the houses and barns, and interacting with staff dressed in authentic costumes was informative and inspiring. Their bookstore offered many books necessary for my research.

I could not afford to purchase every helpful book I needed. I wish to thank the Fryeburg Public Library for providing me with the books for this project and for nineteen years of homeschooling! I could not have done it without them.

Herbalist Carolynn Plowden of Stow, Maine spent a morning with me drinking mint tea and describing the medicinal uses for many locally grown herbs.

The Fryeburg Historical Society made their books and resources available.

I could not have written this book without the love and support of my family. My sensitive and intelligent son, Timothy was the inspiration for my fictional character, Benjamin Miller. My AMAZING GRACEful daughter, Perry was a model for Grace Peabody's strength, perseverance, charm and love for shoes.

My timber framer and multi-talented husband, Wayne helped write the sections on the geometry lesson, the botany lesson, the timber frame, the frame raising and the basket weaving. Ethan, Micah and James Miller all possessed some of Wayne's skills and abilities. Thank you for encouraging me to embark on this project and for helping me through the rough spots.

About the front cover: The cover photo was shot by Kim Knollenberg of South Tamworth, NH in front of the hearth at Remick Country Doctor Museum and Farm in Tamworth, NH. The authentic, period costume was designed and created by Tonya Ring of Fryeburg, Maine. Thank you to my hairdresser, Kelly Connell of Hair with Flair in Fryeburg for doing Perry's hair "just like the picture". A very special thank you goes to my daughter, Perry, for posing as Grace.

Chronology of Events

1765 - The Stamp Act
John Adams wrote the Braintree Instructions
1766 – The Repeal of the Stamp Act
1770 – The Boston Massacre
The Quartering Act
1771 – The Boston Tea Party
1772 – The Townsend Act
1775 – The Battle of Lexington and Concord
1776 – February - Henry Knox delivers artillery which was captured by Ethan Allen in Fort Ticonderoga to General George Washington in Cambridge, Massachusetts
1776 – March 2 and 3 – General Washington attacks the British in Boston
1776 – March 17 – General Howe and the British fleet leave Boston
1776 – July 4 – The Declaration of Independence is signed
1777 – February – John Adams and his son, John Quincy Adams, leave for Paris
1779 – August – John and John Quincy Adams return to Braintree, Massachusetts
1779 – November – John Adams and two of his sons, John Quincy and Charles return to France
1780 – John Adams and sons leave for Holland

1781 – Summer - John Quincy Adams leaves for Russia

1781 – October 19 – The Battle of Yorktown – General Cornwallis surrenders to General Washington

1783 – September 3 – The Treaty of Paris is signed, officially ending the Revolutionary War.

The Cast of Characters

I n this work, as in all of historical fiction, we have fictional characters interacting with historical figures, observing, reacting and at times participating in actual historical events.

Fictional Characters: James and Sarah Bradford Miller and their children are fictional characters; Sarah Bradford and her parents and siblings are fictional descendants of William Bradford, one of the Pilgrims who arrived on the Mayflower in 1620. William and Elizabeth Peabody and their daughter Grace are also fictional. There were wealthy and influential Peabodys in the Massachusetts Colony at that time period. However, any similarities between the fictional and historical characters are purely unintentional. Elizabeth Alden and her parents and siblings are fictional descendants of Pilgrims John and Priscilla Alden. River View Farm exists only in our imaginations.

The Town's People: Fryeburg, Maine is the oldest town in Oxford Country. The names of the town's people and their occupations are historically correct; Joseph Frye was given the grant of land which became the town of Fryeburg. Reverend William Fessenden was a highly respected early minister of the Congregational Church just as Dr. Joseph Emery was the town's first physician. The Walkers, the Knights and the Osgoods were prominent families during this time period. Caleb Swan, a graduate of Harvard College and a classmate of John Adams, was also a Lieutenant in the Revolutionary War. I cannot guarantee that he was residing at his home in Fryeburg during the last three years of the War. Samuel Osgood did have a slave named Limbo who is buried in the Fryeburg Village Cemetery. One source stated that he was illiterate; I took the literary license and had Benjamin Miller teach him to read and write and Abigail Miller teach him his Bible stories.

National Figures: All the national figures and the events about which Abigail Adams writes in her many letters to Sarah Miller are real. Please see in the appendix the page entitled "Historical Figures".

Historical Figures

Abigail Adams (b. 1744 d. 1818) - wife of John Adams, the second First Lady of the United States and mother of the sixth President, John Quincy Adams

John Adams (b.1735 d. 1826) – a patriot, statesman, diplomat, first Vice President of the United States and the second President of the United States 1797- 1801

John Quincy Adams (b. 1767 d. 1848) – son of John and Abigail Adams who had a distinguished career in serving his country before becoming the sixth President of the United States 1825- 1829

Samuel Adams (b. 1722 d. 1803) an outspoken Patriot, a member of the Sons of Liberty, the second cousin of John Adams, Founding Father and attendee of the Continental Congress

Ethan Allen (b. 1738 d. 1789) farmer, war hero remembered for his capture of Fort Ticonderoga, one of the founders of the state of Vermont

Thomas Chippendale (b. 1718 d. 1779) – a London cabinet maker and furniture designer

John Singleton Copley (b. 1738 d. 1815) – an American artist famous for painting portraits of important figures in Colonial New England such as John Adams, John Quincy Adams, John Hancock, Paul Revere and Samuel Adams

William Dawes (b.1745 d. 17990 – assigned by Dr. Joseph Warren to ride from Boston to Lexington to warn the citizens of the approaching British army.

Euclid (b. 323 BC d. 283 BC) – Greek mathematician, author of Elements and referred to as the Father of Geometry

General Thomas Gage (b. 1719 d. 1787) a British general appointed in 1774 as military Governor of Massachusetts, ordered the British march on Lexington and Concord, replaced by General William Howe after the Battle of Bunker Hill

John Hancock (b. 1737 d. 1793) – wealthy merchant, statesman, President of the Second Continental Congress, best remembered for his prominent signature on the Declaration of Independence

General William Howe (b. 1729 d. 1814) British Army Officer and the Commander-in-Chief of the British armed forces during the Revolutionary War

Thomas Hutchinson (b. 1711 d. 1780) British Royal Governor of Colonial Massachusetts

Henry Knox (b. 1750 d. 1806) – military officer in the Continental Army and U.S. Army, best remembered for transporting the artillery from Fort Ticonderoga to General Washington in Cambridge.

Andrew Oliver (b. 1706 d. 1774) – in 1765 he was commissioned to administer the Stamp Act, his home was ransacked by an angry mob, became Lt. Governor of Massachusetts Colony in 1771.

Captain Thomas Preston (b. 1772 d. 1791) British officer present at the Boston Massacre who was defended by John Adams and acquitted of all charges

Pythagoras (b. 570 BC d. 495 BC) – Ancient Greek philosopher and mathematician best known for his Pythagorean Theorem

Paul Revere (b. 1735 d. 1818) – American silversmith, Patriot and messenger warning Lexington and Concord of the arrival of British troops

Joseph Warren (b. 1741 d. 1775) American doctor who notified Paul Revere of British plans to attack Lexington and Concord

General George Washington (b. 1732 d. 1799) – Commander-in-Chief of the Continental Army and the first President of the United States

Information for the above summaries was gleaned from Wikipedia.

I

The Loss

"Mother, you should not be out here alone," four-teen-year-old Benjamin Miller gently reminded her. He wrapped her black, wool cloak around her thin, frail shoulders to protect her from the February winds.

"I miss her too," he whispered as the two forlorn figures stared at the gravestone before them.

Abigail Elizabeth Miller
Beloved Daughter of James and Sarah Miller
Born February 2, 1767
Died December 24, 1780

Abigail, Benjamin's twin, was named after Sarah's two childhood friends back in Weymouth, Abigail Smith and Elizabeth Alden.

Benjamin's muffled cough betrayed his own recent ill-ness. "Mother, it is beginning to snow. Father will be worried if he discovers you are not home."

"No, we must not worry your poor father—not after what he has been through."

Benjamin slipped his arm around her waist and gingerly led her around the patches of ice as they left the village cemetery[1]and began to descend the ridge to their farm.

"Father!" Micah ran breathlessly into the barn. "Have you seen Benjamin? Half the sheep are out of the pen and one is on the bank of the Saco."

James sighed as he put down his mallet and chisel. "Ethan, go help Micah round up the sheep." Ethan opened his mouth to protest, and then thought better of it.

"Yes, sir," he mumbled. The brothers exchanged knowing glances before heading out the door.

"Why cannot Benjamin be more like his brothers?" James slowly shook his head. Seventeen-year-old Micah thrived facing the challenges and responsibilities each season brought to their northern New England farm. Micah did not just plant crops - he studied them, making careful records of rainfall, hours of sunlight and soil conditions. He was a problem solver. When deep snows prevented them from tapping their maple trees three years ago, he made snowshoes like the Indians. When the children outgrew their leather boots, he made knee-length, deer skin moccasins lined with rabbit fur. At six feet tall and broad shoulders, reddish brown hair and blue eyes, he was the spitting image of his father.

Even at the age of twelve, Ethan was a talented carpenter. Six years ago he began making simple furniture like stools and benches. The two of them were now cutting the timbers for an addition to their barn to be completed before planting.

But what should James do with Benjamin? He and Abigail, born too early and too small, were fragile as young children always the first to get sick and the last to recover.

The Millers, like the other families in Pequawket, taught their children at home. Sarah was teaching seven-year-old Micah to read from the dog-eared copy of the New England Primer, when four-year-old Benjamin grabbed the book and began to read out loud. When Abigail struggled to learn her letters, he became her private tutor, protector and defender.

Five-year-old Abigail was terrified of the ornery hen that would peck at her when she tried to collect the eggs. Hearing his sister's screams one morning, he rushed into the hen house, grabbed the offending fowl, snapped its neck and exclaimed, "Let that be a lesson to anyone else who attacks my sister."

James explained to his son, "You cannot kill an animal out of anger. It is one thing to hunt or to slaughter one of the pigs to provide food for the family, but you are to never kill out of anger." To reinforce the lesson, he applied the switch three times to Benjamin's little bottom as Abigail sobbed in the corner. He took it like man, put his hands on his hips and said, "I do hope you're satisfied. You have terribly unsettled my sister."

Benjamin read before, after and instead of doing chores. He read by daylight, moonlight, firelight or candlelight. Yet, a father had an obligation to teach his sons a trade. A man cannot provide for a family by reading books!

He sighed once more as he left the warmth of the barn and headed toward the house. Looking up toward the little graveyard he saw mother and son in the distance, slowly walking arm in arm. "How did this happen?" he asked himself in bewildered despair.

Just October the Millers had invited the Swan family for a harvest supper. The aroma of venison stew simmering in the large black pot hanging in the fieldstone hearth filled the room. There was much talking and laughter around the 12 foot pine trestle table as they passed baked acorn squash, smoked ham, turnips and buttered cornbread. The children drank their apple cider while the adults savored their second cup of syllabub.

"A toast," Caleb Swan stood up holding his cup. "To friendship."

James and Caleb were friends since they met at Harvard College. It was Caleb who told him about the fertile farmland in the intervale of the Saco River and the forest rich with pine, spruce, hemlock, birch, maple, oak and poplar trees. The fields were filled with wild blueberries, cranberries, black berries and raspberries. Acres of this Garden of Eden were for sale in the new township called Pequawket, the very first town in the White Mountains.[2]

Colonel Joseph Frye was granted this land for serving with distinction in the French and Indian War. After Caleb married Colonel Frye's sister, Dorothy in 1763 and began his own homestead, he wrote several letters to James urging him to move up north and share in the adventures.

How could he? Had not the Lord called him to the ministry? He could not just leave his small Congregational Church in Cambridge to become a farmer. What about Sarah and two-year old Micah? Sarah and her older sister Esther visited each other several times a week. Sarah still remained close to her family and friends back in Weymouth. She could not just pull up roots to live on an isolated farm miles from loved ones.

In the spring of 1765 James received a visit from attorney John Adams from Braintree who informed him that he had inherited money from his uncle Benjamin. John, a fellow Harvard classmate who had recently married Sarah's dear friend Abigail, stayed for supper. They spent that evening discussing the financial impact the Stamp Act will have on the colonists when it would take effect in November.

The next morning Sarah told him, "I think you should do it. I think the Lord has now provided you with the money to go buy that farmland."

"Are you sure?"

"I can be a poor farmer's wife as easily as I can be a poor pastor's wife," she teased.

"But what about my ministry?"

"I imagine that Pequawket has sinners just as Cambridge does."

James smiled warmly back at Caleb. "To friendship." The Lord had blessed him with a Godly wife, four healthy children, good friends, their own home, plenty of food and firewood to last until next spring.

Was that evening only four months ago? It seemed like a lifetime ago...

It started as a cough and a cold. James took little notice because Abigail was often sick and Sarah would nurse her back to health. Autumn is a busy time for a farmer and his family if they were to survive the harsh winter.

The coughing continued into November. Sarah utilized all of her knowledge of herbal remedies which her mother had taught her. First she gave Abigail three cups of horehound tea per day for the cough. When Abigail failed to improve, Sarah tried Echinacea tea three to four times a day to battle colds and flus. Now Sarah grew alarmed when cups of hyssop tea failed to alleviate the cough and the accompanied respiratory distress.[3] Abigail was now confined to her bed in the small first floor bedroom next to theirs.

Benjamin grew equally alarmed over his sister's condition. In addition to doing Abigail's chores of feeding the chickens and caring for the sheep as well as his own chores, Benjamin spent hours by her bedside reading to her.

In late November the unthinkable happened; Sarah suddenly fell ill. James felt totally helpless as he sent for Dr. Emery. "I do not like the sound of that cough," he shook his head. "Keep the boys away from them." Sarah insisted that Abigail sleep with her in their big bed, so she could tend to her daughter.

Benjamin made a gallant attempt in taking over the cooking. He had his grandmother's hasty pudding recipe memorized by watching his mother cook breakfast each morning. He methodically lined up the ingredients on the table:

1 cup cornmeal
1 quart water
½ teaspoon of salt
Molasses
Milk
Butter

He then placed the water and salt in a pot hanging on the crane and swung the pot over the flames in the hearth. When the water began to boil, he slowing added handfuls of cornmeal with his left hand while constantly stirring the pot with a large wooden spoon with his right. He took pride that there were few if any lumps in his pudding. He knew if the wooden spoon could stand upright by itself in the middle of the pot, the pudding was ready. He would swing the pot away from the flames to add milk, molasses and butter[4]

For the light evening meal he would melt butter or lard in a hanging griddle over a moderate fire before adding slices of cold leftover hasty pudding. Experience taught him how long it took one side to brown before flipping them over to brown the other side. These meals could be augmented with fried apple slices and washed down with mint tea or cider.

However, it was dinner, the large mid-day meal that Benjamin could not master. There was simply no time to prepare a meal while feeding the chickens, collecting eggs, caring for Mother and Abigail, cleaning up from breakfast, feeding the sheep, bringing in firewood and bringing in buckets of water from the well. Although Micah and Ethan did help out the best they could, the four Miller men were constantly hungry.

Sarah made everything she did look effortless. How did she manage all this in addition to teaching the children, doing the laundry, the spinning, the weaving, sewing, mending, caring for the kitchen garden, making soap and candles?

Benjamin had a solution. While mother and daughter slept and father and sons were out in the barn, Benjamin quickly filled a sack with root vegetables, cornmeal, lard, salt pork, beans, butter, dried apples and sausages, then rode off on their horse, Aristotle.

"Where have you been?" James demanded when his son returned. I am worried enough about your sister and mother and you take off with the horse without permission!"

"I was visiting Mrs. Osgood, Mrs. Bradley and Mrs. Swan to ask them if they would cook our dinners for us."

"You did what? Millers do not ask for charity!"

"We have to eat, do we not? Besides I gave them plenty of food to cook for our family as well as their own. That is not charity. That is bartering." he explained.

During the third week of December, James told Ethan to take Aristotle to deliver two sealed letters - one to Samuel Osgood and one to Caleb Swan. He returned later that afternoon with a small leather pouch with nails from Mr. Osgood and a message from Mr. Swan, "Tell your father I shall get working on it right away."

"Ethan, come to the barn with me and help me plane these pine boards please."In the early hours of December 24 the brothers were awakened by their mother's screams. Abigail's coughing had stopped.

On Christmas Day James and his three sons took the planed pine boards and the nails and lovingly built Abigail's coffin as Dr. Joseph Emery and Rev. William Fessenden tended to Sarah who was delirious with fever. Caleb delivered the hand-carved granite gravestone to the village cemetery.

The next day the entire town of Fryeburg, except Dr. Emery who stayed with Sarah, attended the funeral.

Four days later, Sarah's fever broke and she began to ask for Abigail. She could not believe her daughter, her constant companion, was gone. James hitched Aristotle to the wagon,

25

bundled Sarah up in quilts, and took her to the cemetery to see Abigail's gravestone for herself. Later James returned the small leather pouch with the rest of the nails to Samuel.

James had hoped that the worst was behind them. The second week in January Benjamin collapsed in the door yard while carrying an armful of firewood. Sarah flew out of the house barefooted in her bed clothes, threw herself upon Benjamin screaming," You took my Abigail but I shall never let you take my Benjamin! Never! Never!" she blasphemed.

Shaken at his mother's outburst, Ethan ran to the barn and cried. Micah felt like following him, but he was a man now and he could not be seen crying like a little girl. James picked up Sarah and lovingly returned her to bed. Micah picked up his brother, placed him in Abigail's little bed and ran to get Dr. Emery.

"He has exhaustion," the doctor declared, "and a bad cold. He needs plenty of rest."

"And a few books to read," Benjamin whispered.

"Thank you for caring for your mother. You are a good son, Benjamin," James squeezed his slender shoulder. Benjamin blushed at his father's praise. "I shall take her from here," he swept Sarah into his arms and carried her back into the house.

II

The Letters

James glanced around their home in dismay as he gently placed his wife in the oak rocking chair by the hearth and wrapped her in the quilt from their bed. The house was cold, dark and untidy. Three large, square willow baskets filled with uncarded fleece lined one wall. Sarah's spinning wheels stood silently in a corner collecting dust.

"Micah, please tend the fire. Benjamin, please heat some water for washing, and put the tea pot on the trivet over the coals." James handed Ethan the willow broom, "Please begin sweeping and don't forget the corners," he instructed as he gathered the dirty dishes from the pine table.

"Can someone please explain to me why four grown men cannot do the work of one woman?" Ethan complained. James chuckled as Sarah returned his gaze and smiled.

How James missed his plump, rosy cheeked wife with the smiling dark brown eyes. The frail, pale woman with the dark circles under her sad eyes quietly rocked and sipped her mint tea.

It was those big brown eyes that caught his atten-tion almost twenty years ago. Seventeen- year- old Sarah Bradford, the youngest of seven children from Weymouth,

27

quietly entered church one Sunday morning with her eldest sister Esther, Esther's husband John and their six children. James stumbled three times while preaching his sermon because of those big brown eyes.

She had recently moved in with her sister and family to help care for their ever growing brood. John, an elder of the church, often invited the twenty-six year old, single minister to his home for family dinners and discussions of church matters. Just one visit revealed that Sarah was no ordinary young woman. She was an accomplished seamstress and weaver, a good cook and as industrious a homemaker as any of her older sisters. She was also as well read and knowledgeable in literature, history, theology and politics as any of her older, Harvard-educated brothers. She had read nearly every book in her father's formidable library.

It took James almost a year to summon his courage to ask Mr. Bradford for his daughter's hand in marriage. In the spring of 1762 they were wed at the Bradford home in Weymouth surrounded by her large extended family and two best friends, Abigail Smith and Elizabeth Alden. He had made a covenant before God to love and cherish his wife in sickness and in health. He intended to honor that commitment.

After they cleaned the first floor of the house, they ate a dinner of Mrs. Swan's reheated sausage, fried potatoes with onions and squash pie. Benjamin and Ethan washed and dried the dishes, put the dishes back in the pine cupboard, and hung the towel by the fire to dry. James instructed, "Micah, please feed and water the livestock and milk the cow." In addition to naming the two horses Aristotle and Socrates, Abigail named the cow Athena. However, James always referred to Athena as "the cow."

"Ethan, let us get back to work on that barn frame while we still have daylight. Benjamin, please read Mrs. Adams' and Mrs. Peabody's letters aloud to Mother. You would enjoy that, would you not, Sarah?"

Benjamin lifted the lid of the white pine chest where Sarah's treasured letters were neatly tied up in a blue ribbon for Mrs. Adams' letters and a white ribbon for Mrs. Peabody's.

"Mother, Abigail is gone. She is not coming home. That is why I feed the chickens and care for her sheep. I think it is time," Benjamin brought over one basket of fleece and Abigail's carding combs."

With trembling hands, Sarah silently put a handful of fleece in her lap and picked up the two combs. Benjamin untied the blue ribbon and took the top letter. Benjamin loved hearing about the unfolding events in Boston and the hardships endured by its citizens as the War for Independence progressed. At Sarah's insistence he also untied the white ribbon and placed Elizabeth Peabody's letters on the pine table.

December 1765
Braintree, Massachusetts

My Dearest Sarah,

Your brother Jacob stopped by the house last week and told us all about how James, Caleb Swan and he built your home this summer. He still has the calluses on his hands from hauling the fieldstones for your hearth and chimney. He has assured me that you and Micah arrived safely in Pequawket in October, your home is solid and sturdy and you will be well sheltered this winter. The countryside sounds both majestic and tranquil.

Events in Boston have been anything but tranquil. The Stamp Act went into effect last month. Everything written on paper such as books, newspapers, legal documents require revenue stamps. The British are taxing us to recoup the expenses of the French and Indian War and attempting to establish a military presence in the colonies. Just recently a Boston mob stoned the residence of Andrew Oliver, the Secretary of the Province and destroyed the home of Lieutenant Governor, Thomas Hutchinson[1]

I am enclosing a copy of a pamphlet which John has penned called the 'Braintree Instructions'. He says," we have always understood it to be a grand and fundamental principle of the English Constitution that the freeman should not be subject to any tax to which he has not given his own consent."[2]

Speaking of the lack of tranquility I am pleased to tell you that our first child is a daughter named Abigail whom we shall call Nabby. I must close for now, for Nabby has awakened. I am most anxious to hear from you.

> *Affectionately,*
> *Abigail Adams*

September 1766
Boston, Massachusetts

Dear Sarah,

Your friend Elizabeth is no longer an old maid. Mr. William Peabody proposed marriage in May and I accepted his offer. We were married in William's parents' home on Beacon Hill and had an elegant reception in the gardens. Everyone you know was there including Abigail, John and baby Nabby. Abigail's father Rev. Smith performed the wedding ceremony.

I do hope you will not be scandalized that I have married a man twenty-five years my senior. I must tell you that marrying a gentleman firmly established in business and in society provides many advantages.

Father Peabody has been too generous. He has offered William a partnership in his shipping business, a clipper ship of his very own christened The 'Sweet Elizabeth' and a lovely home just two doors down from them. Of course it is nothing as grand as John Hancock's home, but then nothing is.

I must tell you I could not possibly manage such an elaborate household without the help of six servants. Do forgive my brevity. William is leaving next week for Philadelphia and I must begin to dress for a reception being held in our honor this evening.

Fondly,
Elizabeth Alden Peabody

December 1766
Braintree, Massachusetts

My Dearest Sarah,

I thank Providence for your health and prosperity this past year. Is it possible that Micah is already three years old? It must be exhausting expecting your second child while trying to keep up with Micah and all the responsibilities on the farm. You say that this pregnancy feels much differently from your first. Please try to get some rest.

Yes, I agree that our humble farmhouses will never be as elegant as Elizabeth's mansion, but may they be furnished with love, humility and good tidings.

Elizabeth was indeed a beautiful bride and the food was simply delectable. John had two servings of stuffed pheasant and three slices of bourbon pecan cake. My parents and sisters were in attendance but oh how I wished you were there!

Please write Elizabeth as soon as you have the opportunity. She is rather lonely since William went to sea last month. I fear she is realizing that silk draperies, china and crystal do not make warm company.

31

I have noted that I must change your address from Pequawket to Fryeburg. Fryeburg is a good and proper name for a town of good and proper people. Colonel Joseph Frye does indeed deserve the recognition for his energies in establishing this township. Pequawket always sounded more like an Indian village.

Have you heard that they have repealed the Stamp Act?[3] That is a sweet victory for the colonies.

Nabby will be having a brother or sister sometime this summer. Someone is at my door so I must close for now. I am most anxious to hear from you.

> *Affectionately,*
> *Abigail*

January, 1767
Boston, Massachusetts

Dear Sarah,

Thank you for your kind letter and warm wishes. You are in my thoughts and prayers as you await the birth of your second child.

William returned from Philadelphia on 'The Sweet Elizabeth' at the end of December. I must tell you my husband is much too generous! He brought home two chests of Bohea Tea from the Wiyi Mountains in the Fujian Province in China, an exquisite porcelain tea set, and bolts and bolts of silk. He says now that I am a Peabody I must learn to entertain like one. I will be hosting several functions in my home this winter. Mother Peabody has graciously offered to supervise the preparations.

William will be home until the end of April. I fear the time will pass too quickly while he is here and too slowly once he is gone.

> *Fondly,*
> *Elizabeth Alden Peabody*

September, 1767
Braintree, Massachusetts

My Dearest Sarah,
 The year 1767 has been an exceptional year for the "Girls from Weymouth". Your mother told me you had been blessed with twins. I am so honored that you named your daughter Abigail after me. She also told me that Abigail and Benjamin are very delicate and that you feared for their little lives. I thank Providence that they are growing and appear to be healthy. I now understand why you have not written recently.
 On July 7, I gave birth to our first son, John Quincy Adams.[4] Nabby is not sure what to make of her little brother. I am afraid that John has spoiled her with his affections and she may not appreciate sharing those affections with John Quincy.
 Last week our dear friend Elizabeth had a daughter named Grace Alden Peabody. When we played together as children did you ever dream that the three of us would someday be mothers?
 I must close for John Quincy is wailing to be fed and Nabby is into mischief once again. Promise me you will write me soon for I am most anxious to hear from you.
 Affectionately,
 Abigail

May, 1768
Boston, Massachusetts

My Dearest Sarah,
 Please note the change of address. John's legal practice in Boston has become so busy; he rented a home for us here so he could see more of the family.[5]

Have you heard from Elizabeth? I visited her twice last month. The poor girl appears to be overwhelmed with the demands of motherhood while William is away. Grace is a beautiful baby but is most colicky. I encouraged her to cheer up, colic will soon pass.

British troops are everywhere. I cannot go to market without seeing at least a dozen red coats. John says since the British passed a new round of taxes on paper, tea, paint and glass, they need the troops to keep order. They wish to avoid the vandalism which resulted in the passing of the Stamp Act.

In a few months I will also be a mother of three. When you write to Elizabeth, please do not mention this to her just yet.

I was relieved to receive your letter last month and learn that Abigail and Benjamin are doing better. It sounds like Micah will grow up to be a farmer. Almost five years old and he is helping James with the planting! I must close. Nabby is pulling the cat's tail again and someone is at the door.

Abigail

September, 1769
Boston, Massachusetts

Dear Sarah,

I beg your forgiveness for not writing sooner. Two year old Grace is quite a handful. Our governess can barely keep up with her.

Did you hear that Abigail had another girl last year? She named her Susannah. Now I hear that you have had your fourth child! I am sure your mother was pleased that you named him Ethan after your father. I simply do not know how you and Abigail manage all those children and no household help.

I must tell you I am at my wit's end. John Hancock is holding a reception at his home tomorrow evening. I have

*been in dress fittings all week and William is two weeks over
due at sea. Mother Peabody says I should go alone. Where
else in Boston could I wear such an extravagant dress of
gold brocade? However, I do not think it is proper for a lady
to attend such an event without a proper escort. What would
people say?*

*Yesterday three trunks filled with books, a tall clock,
an armoire and a desk designed and built by Thomas
Chippendale arrived from London. As I am writing I have
workers traipsing up and down the back staircase building
bookcases, converting an extra bedroom into a small library.
What else could I do? There is simply no shelf space or
room for additional furniture left in William's drawing room
downstairs.*

*Last week I had Abigail and the children over for tea. I
was so pleased that Grace and John Quincy played so nicely
together. It appears that John Adams is developing quite a
successful law practice in Boston.*

*William's carriage has just pulled up to the front door. I
do believe I shall be attending Mr. Hancock's reception after
all.*

*Please write soon. I do enjoy reading about your little
farm in the wilderness.*

> *Fondly,*
> *Elizabeth Alden Peabody*

Benjamin put down the letters. "Mother, you are smiling."

"Yes dear. I have always found Elizabeth's letters to be
amusing. Please keep reading while I make us another pot
of tea."

"Is the tea imported?" Benjamin joked.

"Why yes, sir. The leaves from the raspberry bushes
have been imported all the way from our field through the
back door," she smiled. "Do keep reading. I have plenty of
fleeces left to card."

April, 1770
Boston, Massachusetts

Dear Sarah,

I must tell you it is simply not safe for a lady to step out her front door. I do not know who are worse - the hoodlums who call themselves the Sons of Liberty or the undisciplined British troops patrolling our streets harassing decent citizens.

Well, the night of March 5 an unruly mob of 300-400 people approached the Custom House on King Street. There was only one British sentry on duty. Some British soldiers came to his aid, one thing led to another. The mob was shouting, cursing, throwing snowballs, chunks of ice and rocks. The British troops fired into the crowd killing three civilians instantly and wounding eleven more, two who later died.[6]

Samuel Adams is calling this a "bloody butchery." I do not know how Abigail tolerates that man. I know Samuel and John are only second cousins, but he is tarnishing the Adams' good name.

You can imagine how frightening it would be to be a woman alone with a young child while her protector is hundreds of miles away at sea. I am never sure where William is or when he will return or if he will return at all.

Do you know who volunteered to defend these British soldiers? John Adams.[7] Father Peabody says this could ruin his reputation, not to mention his career.

Obviously John's successful legal practice is not prohibiting him from performing his husbandly duties. Do you know Abigail is expecting another baby this summer?

I barely can keep all of these children straight. Micah must be 7 years old; Abigail and Benjamin three years old and Ethan one year old. Are there any more little Millers on the way?

I must leave for tea with Mother Peabody. She wants me to have my portrait painted by John Singleton Copley as a birthday gift for William.
> *Fondly,*
> *Elizabeth*

> *September 1770*
> *Boston, Massachusetts*

My Dearest Sarah,

I beg your forgiveness for not replying sooner. This has been a trying time. John works tirelessly on the defense of Captain Thomas Preston and the British soldiers accused of killing five civilians at what Paul Revere calls the "Boston Massacre". Although I whole heartedly agree with John that "no man in a free country should be denied the right to counsel and a fair trial," the threats to my dear husband and our family are most distressing.[8]

Our fourth child and second son, Charles was born this summer.[9] John has been elected as a representative to the Massachusetts legislature. The children rarely see their father these days.

Nabby and John Quincy loved the story about your friend, John Dresser. Imagine having twenty Indians camping in the kitchen, sleeping on the floor and cooking in their fireplace! [10] They cannot believe that Micah and Benjamin actually played in the yard with some of the Indian children.

I will write again in a few months. Captain Preston's trial is scheduled in October and the trial for the remaining soldiers in December.

The tensions between the British troops and the Boston citizens increase daily. There is much resentment that many of the troops are being quartered in private homes. I fear taking the children with me to market, but I must not give in to my fears.

John Quincy says he would much rather have Indians in his front yard than lobster backs.
Affectionately,
Abigail

January, 1771
Boston, Massachusetts
Dear Sarah,
I must tell you that John Adams is probably the most popular man in Boston, if not the entire colony. William and Father Peabody attended both the trial of Captain Preston and the trial of the other British soldiers. They say it was positively riveting. Captain Prescott was acquitted.

We had an exquisite dinner party for William's birthday. He simply loved my portrait. He declared it was breathtaking. John Hancock said it was a true likeness.

Mother Peabody has been feeling poorly. Therefore I have assumed the role of hostess at their home as well as my own.

Father Peabody is relinquishing all the financial responsibility of the firm to William. It is a huge undertaking and William spends day and night at the counting house. I do hope this means he will spend less time at sea. It is such a comfort to have him home. Three year old Grace barely knows her father. Just last week she called one of the grooms-men "Papa". I must tell you I was simply mortified.
Fondly,
Elizabeth Alden Peabody

Benjamin put down the letters. Oh how he would have loved to have been in that courtroom! Imagine having a famous attorney for a father. How exciting it would have been to be part of the crowd outside of the Custom House.

Nothing exciting ever happens in Fryeburg. Benjamin would love to live in Boston, to see British soldiers in their scarlet uniforms drilling in Boston Common, to smell the salt air and to watch the ships pull into Boston Harbor, to drink real imported tea with John Hancock or sit in a tavern listening to speeches of Sam Adams and the Sons of Liberty.

How exciting is it to watch corn grow, or to feed the smelly animals or to chop the never ending supply of firewood? He sighed loudly.

October 1772
Braintree, Massachusetts
My Dearest Sarah,

I must ask for your forgiveness for allowing two years to pass since my last correspondence!

John was indeed most successful in defending Captain Prescott and the British soldiers. The aftermath was quite extraordinary and John has obtained numerous and wealthy clients such as John Hancock. Although John is not a respecter of persons for he would serve a poor client as well as a rich one.[11]

Please note the change of address. We have returned to our home in Braintree. After the excitement of living in Boston last year, the peace and tranquility of Braintree is most welcomed. As much peace and tranquility a mother of five children can have. Yes, I did say five. Thomas Boylston Adams was born last month.[12]

Have the good citizens of Fryeburg been impacted by the Townsend Act? Well, brew yourself a pot of mint tea for James and yourself and I shall enlighten you with the latest mischief of our esteemed King George and his Parliament.

In their never ending search for creative ways to exact new revenues from the colonies, tea merchants now must pay the Townsend Duty of three pence per pound of imported tea from England. The East India Trading Company may not trade directly with the colonies. First they sell it to merchants in England who in turn, set sail to Charlestown, Philadelphia, New York and Boston[13]

However, they sadly underestimated the will of the colonists. We are boycotting the imported tea. To do otherwise, would allow Parliament to violate our right to be taxed only by our own representatives.

I shall admit that Labrador Tea is an acquired taste. This evergreen plant grows bountifully in the wild and is available year round. I shall experiment mixing dried mint leaves with it.

The Townsend Act has made our dear friends, William and Elizabeth enormously wealthy. William has no qualms about traveling to Amsterdam to buy ships' worth of untaxed tea from the Dutch, smuggle the contraband to ports in Charlestown, Philadelphia and New York, selling it far below the price of the legally imported tea and making huge profits. [14] William does not dare attempt to smuggle it into Boston Harbor for he is too well known and Father Peabody is a close friend with Governor Thomas Hutchinson.

Besides, William has discovered that there is much money to be made from building and selling slave ships. Elizabeth will protest that the Peabodys are not involved in the slave trade, because they personally do not have slaves or directly purchase and sell them. Does not the building the ships for others to make a living of selling poor souls make them just as guilty?

> *Affectionately,*
> *Abigail*

May 1773
Boston, Massachusetts

Dear Sarah,

I must tell you we have outgrown our little home. William bought us a three story house directly across from Boston Common before he left for Europe two months ago. I fear that I may not see him again until September or October. I will spend that time redecorating and furnishing the house.

Father Peabody is building a new ship. It will be called 'The Amazing Grace'! The Amazing Grace is William's nickname for our precocious daughter.

I have not seen or heard from Abigail since she moved to Braintree. Do write soon, I do enjoy hearing about the adventures of your little family. There are many nights by the fire, I reminisce about our girlhood back in Weymouth. .

Sincerely,
Elizabeth
\

January 1774
Braintree, Massachusetts

My Dearest Sarah,

I do not know if word has reached Fryeburg as to what transpired in Boston in December. Cousin Samuel reported on the events but swears he did not plan it. In late November the ship 'Dartmouth' arrived in Boston Harbor filled with tea. On November 29 thousands of citizens filled the South Meeting House.

Sam passed a resolution to urge the Captain of the Dartmouth to send the ship back to England without paying the import duty. This was not an unreasonable request. The consigners of tea in Charleston, South Carolina were forced to resign and the unclaimed tea was seized by Customs Officials. In Philadelphia, Dr. Benjamin Rush urged citizens to oppose the landing of the tea. When the consigners resigned, the tea was returned to England. In New York City, the consigners also resigned and the ships returned to England with their cargo.

However, Governor Hutchinson held his ground and convinced the tea consigners, two of whom were his sons, not to back down. At this meeting Sam assigned twenty-five men to watch the ship and prevent the tea from being unloaded. Governor Hutchinson refused to grant permission for the' Dartmouth' to leave Boston without paying the duty.

In December two more ships, 'The Eleanor' and 'The Beaver' filled with tea arrived in Boston Harbor. On December 16 seven thousand people gathered at the Old South Meeting House for a second meeting. At this time a small group of men left, disguised themselves as Mohawk Indians, headed for Griffin's Wharf, boarded the three ships and dumped all 342 chests of tea into the sea. Neither the ships themselves nor their crew members were harmed. After all, their quarrel was not with the captain and his men, but with the British Parliament who passed these irksome and meddlesome resolutions.[15] I fear this unfortunate episode may unleash an unseen chain of events. May this letter find you and yours in good health.

Affectionately,
Abigail

Benjamin put down the letter and commented, "That was rather ingenious disguising themselves as Indians."

"Some may say brave and ingenious; others may say cowardly and deceitful. Please continue reading," Sarah encouraged.

May 1774
Boston, Massachusetts

Dear Sarah,

Does that miscreant, Samuel Adams, have any idea of the monetary value of 90,000 pounds of tea?! Over 10,000 British pounds sterling!

Now the British have closed Boston Harbor to all incoming and outgoing ships. William is in Philadelphia and unable to return home to his family.

Last week forty, filthy British troops moved into my new home. Enraged at this indignity, I demanded a meeting with General Thomas Gage who assured me that the Quartering Act makes this outrage perfectly legal. How dare he treat a Peabody like some common shopkeeper!

I told him that troops may take over my home but they shall never get the family silver. I must tell you I spent two exhausting days instructing the servants in packing the books, the china, the sterling silver, the pewter, my portrait, the Chippendale furniture, our clothing, and our bedding. I personally took down the silk draperies and packed them in our trunks. I smuggled packages of tea with my petticoats. I gambled that even General Gage would not stoop to violate a lady's privacy.

Bereft of home, hearth, husband, protector and provider, six-year-old Grace and I moved in with Father and Mother Peabody. How I envy you, Sarah Miller with your loving James by your side every night.

Abigail resides in the relative safety of Braintree. I hear that John has been elected to the Continental Congress and will soon be leaving for Philadelphia. I do hope he can find William while he is there.

My fears for the future grow daily. What shall become of us?

Elizabeth

May 1775
Braintree, Massachusetts

My Dearest Sarah,

I do not know if you have heard of the fighting which took place between the British troops and the Colonial Militia on April 19.[16] I am writing to assure you that John went to Lexington and Concord to survey the damage and met with your brother Jacob. Although he was involved with the shooting in Lexington he was not harmed.

John Hancock and Cousin Samuel were forced to leave Boston for fear of arrest by the British. They sought safety with Mr. Hancock's relatives in Lexington, not far from Jacob's farm. Joseph Warren sent word through Paul Revere and William Dawes on the night of April 18 that the British were sending 700 troops.

Not even the British need that many men to arrest two Americans. They surmised that the troops must be on their way to Concord to retrieve the ammunition and arms stored in the armory there. Everyone had plenty of advanced notice. The weapons were redistributed to several other locations in surrounding communities. Jacob removed Martha and the children to the relative safety of the woods with food and supplies.

Eighty men from the Lexington Militia, who were waiting for the British arrival, emerged from Buchman's Tavern to gather at the village common. Details are few and often conflicting. I do know that shots were fired and eight colonials were killed. No one can agree who shot the first shot.

The British continued on to Concord. Word spread quickly among the militias; the British troops were greeted with musket fire.

Local militia from the surrounding towns of Acton, Concord, Bedford and Lincoln joined the battle. The fiercest fighting occurred during the British retreat to Boston.[17]

If John has any more information for me to pass on, I will certainly write. Be assured Jacob and Esther's families are safe. Our parents in Weymouth are far from harm's way. I have no other information on the rest of your siblings. Since the fighting, communication has been slow and unreliable.

Please keep all of us in your thoughts and prayers during these trying times.

Affectionately,
Abigail

"Did Uncle Jacob really fight in that battle?" Benjamin inquired of his mother's brother Jacob Bradford.

"I believe that all able-bodied men living in Lexington turned out to defend their homes and families. Poor Martha and the children must have been terrified! Now please continue."

Braintree, Massachusetts
February, 1776

My Dearest Sarah,

I have much to report to you. Last month John had dinner with General and Mrs. Washington in their temporary quarters in Cambridge near Harvard Yard. The following day he continued his journey on to Framingham to witness a most incredible sight. I do believe it was Divine Providence.

Henry Knox had traveled all the way to Lake Champlain to "retrieve the artillery captured by Ethan Allen at Fort Ticonderoga." Unbelievably these men hauled 58 cannons in various sizes back to Cambridge. Can you imagine what General Washington can do with such artillery? [18]

Once again, John has left for Philadelphia. In New York he bought this pamphlet entitled 'Common Sense'. [19] *I have read it several times and I thought you and James may want to read it.*

Once again our farm feels empty with John's absence. I will endeavor to keep myself busy and productive to make the time pass more quickly.

I will write again if there is more news to report. Please keep the children and me in your prayers, as well as General Washington and his troops.

Affectionately,

Abigail

Braintree, Massachusetts

April, 1776

My Dearest Sarah,

I knew you would be most anxious for us when you heard about the fighting in Boston. Please let me assure you that the Lord has protected my family and was with General Washington. This is the only explanation I can give.

I did not sleep the nights of March 2 and 3 for the house trembled around us when the American bombardment of Boston began. General Washington's men managed to move the artillery that Henry Knox originally transported from Ticonderoga, to positions in Dorchester overlooking Boston Harbor and the British fleet. It took hundreds of ox teams and a thousand American troops to get all the cannons into position in just one night.[20]

In addition to the cannons, colonial carpenters built great timber frames into which hay bales were thrust to provide cover. These were then surrounded with barrels filled with earth. The barrels offered extra protection and many were rolled down the hill attacking the British troops.[21] I can only imagine the shock the British must have experienced with this surprise attack.

On Sunday, March 17 John Quincy and I climbed Penn Hill and we could not believe our eyes. We could look down onto Boston Harbor and watched General William Howe and the British fleet abandoning Boston. You may count upwards of one hundred and seventy sails. They looked like a forest[22]

It was surely the work of the Lord and marvelous in our eyes.[23] *How else could you explain our small colonial army defeating the most powerful navy in the world?*

> *Affectionately,*
> *Abigail*

> *Boston, Massachusetts*
> *May 1776*

Dear Sarah,

I must tell you I thought the world was coming to an end! Words fail to describe the terror we endured for over two weeks. Imagine a thunderstorm and earthquake that would not end. The house shook violently - books, vases, china thrown from their shelves. Shattered windows, the dining room chandelier crashed onto the mahogany table below. Broken glass everywhere! I feared Father Peabody would have a heart attack.

It was surreal. A thousand of Boston's best and brightest have fled the city to return to England or to start anew in Nova Scotia.

When deemed safe, Mother Peabody, Grace and I ventured to our home recently vacated by the British. It broke my heart to see the wanton destruction and filth. I am determined to have the house repaired, repainted and all of our private treasures restored before William returns home.

They may break my windows, but they shall never break my spirit!

> *Sincerely,*
> *Elizabeth*

III

More Letters

Braintree, Massachusetts
July, 1776

My Dearest Sarah,
I have just received a letter from John. The delegates
of the Second Continental Congress have declared the colo-
nies' independence from England..."

Benjamin imagined what it would be like to be in the same room with such illustrious and noble men as Benjamin Franklin, Thomas Jefferson, George Washington, John Hancock, Samuel Adams and John Adams. What did it feel like to sign your name to the Declaration of Independence?

Although Benjamin was only nine years old at the time, he clearly remembered the day when Fryeburg learned of this momentous event.

"Sarah, get the children and follow me," James instructed with a mischievous grin. He sauntered to the woodshed, sharpened his axe and headed across the field to the woods.

"Where you headed, James?" Samuel Osgood asked.

"To the King's Pine. Care to join me? "

As word spread through the village that James Miller was headed toward his King's Pine, dozens followed. Some brought their axes to help; others came to watch out of curiosity.

The Eastern White Pine, the tallest of the pine trees in North America, can grow from 150-240 feet tall with trunks free of branches to heights of 80 feet or more.

They were highly valued to build ship masts because of their height, straightness, strength and light weight. Therefore King George wanted to ensure that the very best trees were reserved for official use. He sent his Royal Surveyors to mark the tallest and straightest pine trees with three hatchet marks known as the King's Broad Arrow. This signified the tree could only be harvested and used solely for building ships for the Royal British Army.

Naturally this caused a great deal of resentment among the colonists who felt that the trees were their pines and not the king's. More than a few men chopped down their King's Pine and then made the King's Broad Arrow hatchet marks on a smaller, nearby tree.[1]

James, a God-fearing and honest man had obeyed the law until that day.

The small crowd cheered as James took his first swing of the axe. When he rested, Caleb Swan took a turn, followed by Nathaniel Merrill and Samuel Bradley and thence back to James. The earth shook when the 210 foot tree crashed to the ground.

Sarah proudly stated, "Some men declare their independence with the stroke of a pen; others with a swing of an axe."

That September, James built for Sarah a twelve foot dining table affectionately called the Liberty Table.

Boston, Massachusetts,
May, 1777

Dear Sarah,
I must tell you how sweet it was to be once again reunited with William - even if it was only for a few brief months. Of course William was sick with worry when he learned of the bombardment of Boston and as soon as the British left Boston Harbor, he set sail from Philadelphia for home.

Thankfully, he had the foresight to bring home salt, sugar, flour, meat, molasses, more tea and hard currency. No useless Continental dollars for us. He made certain that we had enough provisions to live comfortably throughout the duration of this dreadful war.

He supervised the restoration of our home. Qualified workers were a scarce commodity unless one was willing to double the wages. There were no shortages of willing workers then.

It was with much foreboding, I bid William farewell. I begged him to stay here with his family until the war ended. We have everything we need and he certainly did not need to risk his life in pursuit of more business.

However, he said that he had urgent business in Philadelphia which could not wait until the war ended.

Have you heard from Abigail recently? Can you believe she is with child again?
Fondly,
Elizabeth

> *Braintree, Massachusetts*
> *October, 1777*

My Dearest Sarah,
    Thank you for your letters of encouragement during this difficult time. Life has been a struggle. Inflation is rampant. The little money we do have is nearly worthless. The necessities of life like sugar, salt, molasses are in great shortage.[2]
    It is my duty as a Patriot to make do from our resources from our farm. I pity those destitute in the cities that do not raise their own crops or livestock. You would be most proud of me for I have been weaving and making the children's clothes. Of course I never hope to be the fine seamstress and skilled weaver as my beloved friend.
    Yes, your mother was correct in her last letter to you. In July I gave birth to a stillborn daughter.[3] John will be returning home from Philadelphia in a few weeks. I pray someday after this war, may our families gather around your Liberty Table and break bread together in peace and prosperity.
> *Affectionately,*
> *Abigail*

> *Braintree, Massachusetts*
> *March, 1778*

My Dearest Sarah,
    Thank you for your encouraging letters, for they are surely a lift to my spirits. Alas, John's return to home was a brief respite between journeys. A few weeks ago John left for Paris taking John Quincy with him.[4] Since we were united in marriage fourteen years ago we have been apart more than we have lived together.

I confess my fears having husband and eldest son making the three thousand mile voyage across the perilous, stormy Atlantic in winter. I dare not think of the danger of British capture. But I must be brave. Many Patriots have made far greater sacrifices than I...

"What's wrong Benjamin?" James asked his eleven year old son.

"Nothing, sir," he lied for he knew his father would never understand.

"Your chores are done, you have Homer's Odyssey unopened in your lap and yet you sit there scowling," he observed.

"It's not fair!" Benjamin blurted. "John Quincy Adams is only ten years old and he gets to go to Paris, to meet Benjamin Franklin to go to boarding school! I never get to go anywhere! There is nothing to do in Fryeburg except watch the snow melt, the grass grow and the leaves fall," he whined.

James sighed. Benjamin knew when his father sighed like that he would be given an extemporaneous sermon. "Do you know what covetousness means?"

"Envy, jealousy," he dutifully responded.

"Do you know why the Ten Commandments stated 'Thou shall not covet'?" Benjamin silently stared at the braided rug beneath his feet. "Coveting sows seeds of discontent. We begin to dwell upon the things we want rather than praising the Almighty for what He has given to us.

Never compare yourself to others, Benjamin James, for you shall either grow proud or envious. Neither is pleasing to the Lord."

November, 1778
Boston, Massachusetts

Dear Sarah,

Your words of comfort and encouragement were well timed. I received your letter two days after Mother Peabody's passing. I must tell you although she had been failing; we were not prepared for the finality of her death.

William left Philadelphia over a month ago and he is long overdue. Father Peabody is overwhelmed in his grief and therefore the details of her funeral have fallen to me in William's absence.

The wait of his return grows tedious and irksome. We live a life of quiet seclusion for there are no more receptions, teas or dinner parties.

Grace's tutors assure me that she is advancing admirably in her studies. However, she misses her dear friend John Quincy and spends hours in the library writing him letters in French.

I must draw to a close for there are many funeral details that require my immediate attention. I eagerly await your next letters for they are always a welcomed diversion from this dreary war.

Fondly,
Elizabeth

Braintree, Massachusetts
May, 1780

My Dearest Sarah,

It has been a long winter indeed. Have you received word from Elizabeth? If not, I fear I must relay heartbreaking news. 'The Sweet Elizabeth' was blown up in Delaware Bay approaching Philadelphia, by the British over two months ago. There was only one survivor, First Mate Edward Smyth, who was taken captive.

Elizabeth will not acknowledge that William is dead, insisting that he will return to her at the war's end. She does not leave her home - her meals are brought upstairs to her room. She sees no one nor speaks to anyone other than Grace and Father Peabody. Worst of all, she has convinced Grace that her father is not dead and will return home soon.

I fear for her health and her stability.

Please keep your dear friends in your prayers for the times are trying our patience. Your letters are like medicine for a weary soul.

Affectionately,
Abigail

Sarah put down the carding combs. "Thank you, Benjamin. Tomorrow I shall write Elizabeth another letter. Even though she does not respond, I like to think my letters may provide her some comfort.

It is getting dark and cold, and I grow weary. Please light the candles and set the table, for your father and brothers will be here soon and they will be hungry.

It may be another simple meal, but we will all eat it together. That is more than Abigail and Elizabeth will do this evening."

Winter evenings around the hearth were once James' favorite pastime. The family would peacefully gather around the warmth and light of the large fieldstone fireplace, each with a project to do. Abigail would card wool, often humming or singing as she worked. Sarah would be seated at her spinning wheel quietly working in a rhythmic motion. Ethan would be weaving baskets or whittling. Micah would be busy mending harnesses, boots or moccasins. Every evening James would read a portion of Scripture from the large leather-bound family Bible. Often Benjamin would read a section from Pilgrim's Progress or another favorite book. The house was filled with talk, laughter, song and prayer. The wind may blow, the snow may fall, but the family was safe and warm together in their little farm house.

Tonight the house was silent. Sarah had retired to bed hours ago. Micah and Ethan were whittling ten-inch oak pegs for the timber frame. James was calculating the number of pegs he would need. Benjamin sat with an unopened book in his lap staring at the fire silently brooding.

"I want to visit my family," his voice broke the silence.

James put down his quill and turned to his middle son. "Your family is right here."

"I mean I want to go to Weymouth to meet my grandparents and see the house Mother grew up in. I want to read all the books in Grandfather's library and eat Grandmother's hasty pudding.

I want to meet Aunt Esther and Uncle John and all my cousins in Cambridge. I want to visit Lexington and hear Uncle Jacob tell how he shot a British soldier in the first battle of the war..."

James interrupted with a chuckle, "Your Uncle Jacob never shot a British soldier. He fired his musket in the general direction of the redcoats, missed everyone and blew a great hole in the stone wall."

Ignoring that last comment, Benjamin continued. "I want to bring mother back to her family. She needs her mother and sisters and best friends to help with her grief. She should be drinking real tea in porcelain teacups with Mrs. Peabody and discussing politics with Mrs. Adams. Mother was born to be a lady, not some farmer's wife," he stated coldly.

Micah and Ethan put down their pegs and stared at their father. Never in their lives would they have dared to speak so disrespectfully.

James took a deep breath and chose his words carefully. "You are a very insightful young man. Yes, your mother does need her family and friends right now. However, it is not safe for her to travel - she is too weak. I could never forgive myself, nor could you, if anything ever happened to her," his voice choked with emotion.

"I hope someday all you boys will meet your family. Ethan, do you know you were named for your grandfather? Benjamin, you are a scholar just like him. The two of you could discuss literature, politics and theology for hours in his library. Micah, you should visit the original homestead in Weymouth, your Uncle Josiah and his sons are now running the farm. Of course your infamous Uncle Jacob has a small farm in Lexington.

You should all be very proud that you are descendants of William Bradford who risked everything to cross the Atlantic in the Mayflower to arrive on an unknown shore in an unknown land. He and his fellow Pilgrims suffered greatly and lost much in the first few years of their settlement. But he did not travel here in search of his own comfort and happiness. His sacrifices were the foundation for the freedom and prosperity of future generations. He looked beyond his own sacrifices for the benefit of his children, grandchildren and their children.

The blood of Pilgrims runs through your mother's veins. She was prepared to make the necessary sacrifices for a better life for her children and grandchildren. At least that's what she told me when she talked me into buying our property up here."

The brothers looked at each other incredulously.

"Sons, we have suffered a great loss. I will never forget nor stop loving Abigail, nor will you. But we are not the only family to suffer heartache and loss. Think of the fathers, sons, husbands, brothers who died fighting for our liberty. Think of their widows and children struggling to survive.

We must be thankful that we have each other, our home, and our safety. Remember circumstances in our lives will change, but the Lord our God never changes, He is the same yesterday, today and tomorrow."

He opened the family Bible to the book of James 1: 2-4. "My brethren, count it all joy when ye fall into divers temptations; knowing this, that the trying of your faith worketh patience. But let patience have her perfect work that ye may be perfect and entire, wanting nothing."

IV

The Geometry Lesson

It was March 1 and James had hoped that three winters' worth of preparation, tree felling, splitting, shaping, hewing and timber framing would soon result in a new barn frame before planting season. Bundles of hand-split wooden roof shingles carefully lined one wall of the barn. Thousands of linear feet of split pine clapboards were stored under cover. Great hewn posts, beams, long top plates carved from some of the Millers' tallest and straightest white oaks and white pines lay stacked on the barn floor. Dozens of oak wind braces were stacked against one wall at the north end of the barn.

James was thrilled when young Ethan displayed an eager interest and natural aptitude in timber framing. He was also thankful for Micah's strength and endurance. It was silently understood that this massive two-and-a-half story barn would be James' legacy to his sons and future generations. At 46 feet by 80 feet, it was much larger than what the farm required now. His sons would one day have sons. They could till and plant twice as many acres, raise twice as many live-stock. Ethan might one day use a portion for a woodworking shop.

The three of them spent a greater part of the morning marking out two long, straight lines on the barn floor that met at a shallow point about 2 feet from the center of the long, east wall. Benjamin's sudden appearance startled them.

"Is anything wrong? Is Mother alright?" James asked in concern.

Benjamin smiled sheepishly. "She told me to come make myself useful. Reverend Fessenden delivered a letter from Mrs. Adams and she would like to, and I quote 'read it in peace'."

James smiled. The day after Abigail's funeral he wrote two long letters - one to Mrs. Adams and one to Mrs. Peabody. He had hoped that her two dear friends, who had endured hardship and loss themselves, would be able to provide the consolation and comfort which he could not.

"Perfect timing. I was just about to send Micah to get you."

"You were?" Benjamin asked in surprise. Micah and Ethan looked at each other quizzically.

James was framing his barn the way his elders had taught him by example: he had first hewn the white pine, chestnut and oak logs by hand into approximately square timbers about the width of his hand at one end and for most of its length, and expanding its depth to about twice that width at the other end. The result was a timber that, when stood up upon its smaller end, roughly resembled an unfinished gun stock standing upon its barrel end.

The tops of these 'gun-stocked posts' would then be able to hold all the intricate cuts of the intersecting members of girts, rafters, and plates with plenty of the wood remaining to keep the post strong and durable. The smaller, bottom end remained only large enough to support all the weight of the frame, all the weight of the livestock, hay, winter snow and any and all other necessary feed and farm equipment.

James well understood that the thousands of years of timber framing history in England, Europe and here in the New World created a shared bed of knowledge passed from generation to generation. He would utilize some of that shared knowledge to build his own timber framed barn that would stand the test of time and weather. In fact, he had been doing that very thing for the last two years.

Out behind the present small barn were stacked 18 great granite slabs, each of which measured about 8 inches across, 24 inches wide, and either 1 ½ or 2 fathoms long, about 8 to 12 feet. These granite slabs were for the barn's foundation, preventing the barn from rising every winter from frost and falling each spring from thaw.

He had also seen many a barn fail due to carelessness of the barn's builders and neglect of the barn's owners. James Miller knew all this simply because he was a New Englander by birth, a farmer by trade, and an experienced timber framer by need.

"Benjamin, you know that we have just completed all the bents and we are ready to lay out the rafters. I have seen you studying Euclid's *Elements*. Do you think you could mathematically derive the length of a rafter from the eave to the peak? Could you determine the points at which purlins should intersect them? What information would you need from us to work out those formulas?

Your brothers and I need a few geometry lessons in how to calculate the lengths of all the members of this roof frame without the laborious marking of line and transferring the timbers in and out of the barn.

Smiling, Benjamin replied in his most grownup voice, "Sir, if I may have an hour or so, I shall return with an answer."

As he turned and scampered off toward the house, James warned, "Do not disturb your mother."

Sarah sat alone in her rocking chair and eagerly broke the wax seal on the back of the envelope.

Braintree, Massachusetts
January 1781

My Dearest Sarah,
Oh how I wish you and I could be together at this time. Sorrow should never be born alone. Together burdens may be shared and comfort may be multiplied.

I was in the midst of writing a letter to you, when I received a letter from your heartbroken James. I know there are no words that can be spoken to comfort you after the loss of your beloved Abigail. I hope this letter finds you regaining your strength and recovering your health.

These are extraordinary times with extraordinary hardships. Be strong, my friend, not for your sake but for the sake of your beloved husband and children and for me.

John's letters are few and far between. Now that he, John Quincy and Charles are in Holland, I hear almost nothing from them.[1] I cherish each and every one of your letters for they are filled with encouragement, wisdom and wit.

Sarah, please forgive me for adding further to your sorrows, but I have just received devastating news. Our beloved Elizabeth died two weeks ago. Apparently she took to her bed complaining of an unbearable headache. The next morning one of the servants found her. I do not know what shall become of poor Grace.

We need to be strong for one another. Our families depend on us.

I am, as always, most anxious to hear from you.

Your Faithful Friend,
Abigail

Sarah took the quill, ink pot and piece of parchment from the pine cupboard and sat down at the Liberty Table. She stared at the fire for a long time before she began to write.

James and his two sons were busily scribing lines that connected scratched marks near the end of a rafter when Benjamin returned with his slate and a piece of chalk. "Please put down your tools and give your brother your attention. It is now time for your geometry lesson," he smiled.

"A traditional timber framed barn has four walls, a peaked roof all along the center, two floors inside and large centered wagon doors in the side," Benjamin began.

"It will be a great 8-bent, 7-bay timber frame, and the largest structure I have personally worked on," James added. "Benjamin, are you familiar with the terms *bent* and *bay*?"

Benjamin shook his head, "No, Sir."

"Ethan, could you explain what a bent is?"

"A bent is simply a building unit. In a timber frame, a bent is a single section of the frame that can be assembled on the ground and raised as a unit. It includes all the posts, the carrying beams that connect them, and the rafters that form the roof spanning the two outside posts. Lying on the ground before being raised, this bent would resemble the outline of the building." He drew a diagram of a large barn bent on Benjamin's slate.

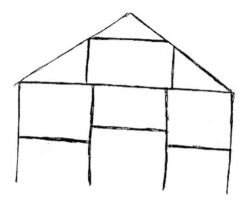

"In our barn frame, each entire bent contains four twenty-foot-long oak posts, a forty-foot white pine girt, a few second-floor girts, and many oak wind braces. With its two white pine rafters, collar ties and queen posts it would be much too heavy for any number of people to raise to a standing position. That is why we will raise the barn as half bents." He adjusted his picture by erasing the roof, adding corner braces, but leaving the square frame otherwise intact.

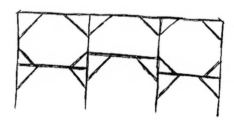

"We will assemble the four posts — two exterior and two interior — with their second and third floor girts and braces to form a large rectangle and then raise just that much.

When they are standing, we peg and secure all these half bents together with wall plates to form the main barn without roof rafters. We will then place enough planks on the topmost floor joists to have footing, or perhaps even floor it over-as much as a barn floor would be. Then we add the rafters with their collar tie connectors and queen posts, assemble them, peg them, and then raise the roof framing. Once all the roof purlins are tapped in to join them, the frame will be complete.

The empty spaces between bents are called the bays. All the bents are locked together with wall plates and wall purlins that span the bays, girts are connected with floor joists and summer beams, and the rafters are connected with roof purlins."

"I could not have explained it better myself, Ethan," approved James.

"Now I understand," Benjamin responded enthusiastically. "Do you want to know the exact length of the rafters in order to cut them all at the same time? The rafters begin at the top of each outside post at the eaves, that is the edge of the barn, and meet its opposite rafter at the peak. If the peak is at the middle, then all roof rafters want to be the same length. Is that not so, Father?" Seeing James' nod, he continued. "If all rafters start at the same place on the outside wall, and they all rise to the peak at the same point, then all will have the same measurement."

"I never thought of doing that," Micah confessed. "But it makes a lot of sense. However, we will not join the rafters to the post tops; we will have a 40-foot-long girt on top of the posts. The rafters will join into these girt ends."

"It does make sense?" Ethan asked.

"Sure," answered Micah enthusiastically. "What we want to lay out correctly is the actual length of each rafter, as well as all the intersecting purlin connection points and all the joinery on it. Although hand-hewn rafters will all have slightly different thicknesses, all their top edges – the barn's roof line, will be at the same level. All the layout points can be marked out also on the top edges. If we can learn all the information we need in order to do this for all the rafters, then we will do this all ahead of time and before any joint is cut."

"We will?" Ethan asked in amazement.

"We just have to custom-fit each rafter foot connection to their girts because the girt ends are also hand-hewn." reminded James

"All we need to know is how far apart the walls are," added Benjamin, "and how high the peak will be and we can find all the rafter lengths. If we know the length for one, then we know the lengths for all. We first determine the lengths of the short sides of a right triangle. "

He rubbed out Ethan's diagram and drew another:

"As you can see, the barn roof forms a simple isosceles triangle."

"What is an isoleez triangle?" Ethan interrupted.

"Not isoleez, isosceles triangle. It is a balanced triangle with two identical sides and two identical angles. If we draw a line straight down to bisect this triangle, we have two right triangles, meaning they have a 90 degree angle in them. This means they have all sorts of properties that other triangles do not have.

"Now we need to apply the Pythagorean Theorem to our known dimensions in order to find the unknown dimensions."[2]

"Wait, I do not understand," Ethan interrupted again. "What theory was that?"

"Pythagoras was an ancient Greek mathematician who is credited with explaining that we can find the long side, called the hypotenuse, of a right triangle by squaring each of the other two sides, adding them together and getting the square root of the sum. The Pythagorean Theorem is stated something like this: 'The square of the hypotenuse of a right triangle is equal to the sum of the squares of the other two sides.' In our case, the hypotenuse is the same as the length of a rafter. Simplified, it mathematically looks a bit like this:"

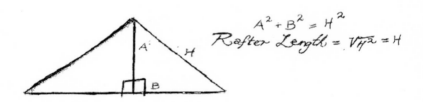

$$A^2 + B^2 = H^2$$
$$\text{Rafter Length} = \sqrt{H^2} = H$$

Ethan was totally baffled. He could not understand how a triangle could have squares.

"That number we are looking for will be the length of the longest side of a right triangle. It works every time without fail. Ethan, carpenters use the Pythagorean Theorem in all sorts of wonderful ways: to determine rafter lengths and the rise and run of stair treads, to determine if a foundation is square, for squaring granite blocks, wagon beds, doors or gates."

Ethan was now determined that he would learn this.

"What is the width of the barn?" Benjamin asked.

"It is 40 feet wide," replied Ethan.

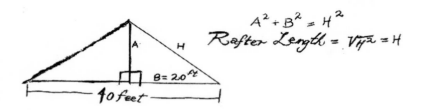

"Because we can safely assume that the peak is the mid-point, then we can divide 40 by 2 and we get 20 feet wide. The length of the bottom side of our triangle, or one-half the width of the barn, is 20 feet."

"When we square this number we will get 400."

"What is the square of a number?" Ethan was getting frustrated.

"It is another way of saying a number multiplied by itself," Benjamin explained. "Two times two is four. Ten times ten is one hundred..."

"And twenty times twenty is four hundred. I understand now."

Benjamin adjusted his diagram again.

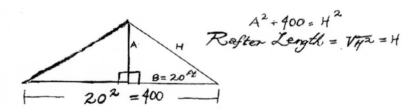

"Father, do you have a designated roof height?"

"Traditionally the English and American builders would choose a rafter length of about 2/3 of the width of any common building. That would give an adequate rise for any purpose. For this barn, let us say that we would like to make the height about 15 feet. What rafter length would that give us?"

"If we take that number 15 as our rise, here on the upright line then square it…"

"I know! I know!" Ethan said excitedly." It is 15 times 15 which equal 225."

"Very good! What is next?" Benjamin asked.

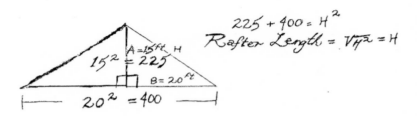

"You need to add 225 to the 400," Micah had no difficulty in following his brother's logic. That would be 625.

"Exactly! Now we need to find the square root of 625 to find the rafter length," Benjamin continued.

Ethan once again was confused. "I can understand how trees have roots. How can squares have roots?"

Benjamin shook his head but Micah explained. "Ethan, what is the square of 2?"

"Two squared is four."

"Therefore the square *root* of four is two."

"I understand! Ten squared is one hundred. The square root of one hundred is ten. Five squared is twenty-five. The square root of twenty-five is five."

"The square root of 625 is 25." Benjamin showed his figuring on his slate. "With a width of 40 feet and a rise of 15 feet the rafters need to be…"

"They need to be 25 feet long. I understand. Because the barn is always 40 feet wide, and the rise is always 15 feet, then every single rafter length will be 25 feet."

Benjamin wrote the number on the slate.

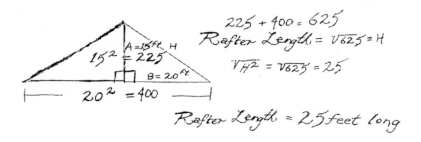

$$225 + 400 = 625$$
$$Rafter\ Length = \sqrt{625} = H$$
$$\sqrt{H^2} = \sqrt{625} = 25$$

$$Rafter\ Length = 25\ feet\ long$$

"I understand," Ethan smiled triumphantly. "Is there more of this useful geometry you can teach me?"

"I believe you will find Euclid's *Elements* to be most relevant." responded Benjamin.

"Is Euclid another one of your dead Greeks?"

"Yes. We can learn a lot of geometry from his book."

"Getting back to the barn," Micah interrupted. "With 25 foot rafters we would have adequate height for the barn roof to store our hay and an adequate slope to shed rain and snow."

Sarah briskly entered the barn with a look of determination and a renewed sense of purpose. "Forgive me for interrupting, gentlemen. James, I need you to post this letter right away."

James rose to receive Sarah's sealed correspondence. "I shall be happy to do so. Boys, measure out and mark the rafter lengths. But do not cut anything until I return and check your work."

"Benjamin, I can show you how, if you would like me to," Ethan offered. The three brothers spent the rest of the afternoon, measuring and marking rafters.

That evening James and all three sons spent considerable time developing geometric formulas for finding the number of purlins, the spacing of all the purlin notches along each rafter and all the locations for every collar tie mortise in the bottom edges of the rafters. Benjamin went to bed tired but content. He was proud that his father needed his help. He did not realize that James already knew all this information; he only knew he felt like part of the family.

V

The Arrival

I t was a cold but sunny March afternoon, as Benjamin and
Ethan snow-shoed south along the Saco River.

"Ethan, I do not think the sap is running yet," Benjamin
nodded toward the sugar maples," the temperature is still too
cold." He knew well that maples need cold nights and warm
days for the sap to run.

"We are not here to tap a tree."

"Then why did you drag me out here?" he asked in
exasperation.

"I want to show you my library", Ethan confided.

Benjamin stopped in his tracks perplexed. "Library? All
I see is the woods."

"Your library has books. My library has trees. You can
learn a lot from trees if you know how to read them."

"Indeed. . . . a most clever analogy," he looked at his
younger brother with a new found respect.

"Thank you," Ethan grinned. "Since you are teaching me
geometry, it is only fair that I teach you about trees. What
kind of tree is this?" he challenged as he pointed to a nearby
evergreen.

"It is coniferous, meaning a tree bearing a cone-shaped
fruit from the Latin *conus*, a cone and *ferre*, bearing."

"It is a hemlock. Do you know how to tell a hemlock from a pine tree?"

"A pine tree has big needles and a hemlock has little flat needles. Plus, the King's agent did not mark any hemlocks with his Broad Axe. At least I do not think he did, did he?"

"No, you are correct. Hemlock wood is no good for masts because it is not as strong and flexible as white pine when it is seasoned. In fact even red pine and spruce is not as good as white pine.

God has designed the most useful tree for just about any purpose when he made the white pine. It is strong yet workable and lightweight. It grows fast around here and I know you have seen some pines well over 100 feet high even in the thickest forest. Its cones are used for food by squirrels and many kinds of birds, and we often use them to quickly start fires even in wet weather."

Benjamin began to look around at more than just the trees as they walked single file. As Ethan spoke about every tree and shrub and grove they strolled past, Benjamin began to notice the black-capped chickadees and red squirrels that darted among the bare branches of the birches, small maples and oaks. While the squirrels occasionally remained silent, the little black and white birds made a constant yet pleasant sound of chirps, peeps and rustling of wings against twigs. Their song of Chick-a-dee-dee-dee brought a smile to Benjamin's face as he imagined them all adding their thoughts to Ethan's lessons.

Ethan pointed out mice trails, with their faint, barely-discernable lines of indentations which abruptly stopped at tiny holes in the snow; fox tracks in single file, making perfectly straight lines; rabbit tracks with the marks of their rear feet way out in front of their smaller front feet; graceful criss-crossing deer tracks; black bear tracks like a man's hand, that occasionally climbed up the trunks of the mature beech trees.[1] Benjamin was absorbing all of this with a new-found

71

interest and enthusiasm, but was also feeling the weariness of the hours-long trek.

"Oh Ethan, how much longer do you plan on keeping me in this library of yours? " After several weeks of illness Benjamin tired easily. 'I do not think I will ever know these woods as you and Father and even Micah seem to. Thank you for showing me your library, but I do not know how to read these books the way you can. And I think perhaps that I will never find the desire to learn how to. I hope that Father will someday accept the fact that I wish not to be a farmer all my life."

"Just like the trees, God has given different people different jobs to do" began Ethan, "Micah is going to be a farmer, I am going to be carpenter and you are going to be a...a..."

"A famous attorney like John Adams."

"A famous attorney."

"We need to head back. The sun is setting behind the western mountains." Benjamin observed.

Unexpectedly Ethan interjected, "Benjamin, I miss her too, you know. Abigail was my friend. Micah is too big-he never wanted to play with me. You are too smart; you never wanted to play with me either. Father and Micah spend all their time together. You and Abigail spent all your time together. Abigail always understood when I felt like I was the black sheep of the family. She'd say, 'Ethan, show me what you're building. Ethan, Come look at Ebony's new lamb. Of all of my sheep, I like the three black sheep the best.' "

"Ethan, you are not the black sheep of the family. I think I am," Benjamin argued.

"If a flock can have more than one black sheep, why can not a family?"

"Another clever analogy. We are Abigail's black sheep and we will both have to stick together," Benjamin patted his younger brother on the back.

"Benjamin, I am glad you did not die."
"Me too, Ethan. Me too."

Micah never minded mucking out the stalls. It was one of the few times his younger siblings didn't pester him and he could think in peace. He could always think more clearly when his hands were busy. He was surprised at how much he missed his sister. Sometimes he feared that the pain and the loss would consume him.

He was proud that, unlike his brothers, he did not cry at the funeral. His father taught him by example that a man remains calm when others panic; a man stays strong when others vacillate. But now the family seemed out of balance with Abigail gone. It was Abigail who named the horses Aristotle and Socrates, the cow Athena and the oxen Hercules and Zeus. It was not fair, the livestock were still there, but she was gone.

Like a mother, she knew the names, personalities, idiosyncrasies and needs of each of her sheep. Ebony, Onyx and Midnight were her three prized black sheep.

One day three summers ago, he was plowing the fields with Hercules and Zeus when he thought he heard a distant cry. Following the sounds, he discovered Abigail in the woods, three quarters of the way up an oak tree where she had climbed to protect a nest of baby robins from a feral cat. After accomplishing her mission, she had frozen in fear as she looked down upon the distant ground.

Climbing to his sister was easy. Climbing down with Abigail on his back, and her arms wrapped tightly around his neck was terrifying. But a man should never display fear. Micah was almost six feet tall even at the age of fourteen.

"Micah, can you get this for me? I cannot reach.
Micah, can you pick me up? I cannot see.
Micah, can you open this for me? It is too hard.

Micah, can you carry me across the puddle? I do not want to get my feet wet.

Micah, can you go to the barn with me? It is getting dark and I am afraid."

Benjamin may have been Abigail's soul mate and Ethan her friend, but Micah was her hero. Now, he was nobody's hero.

Suddenly hot tears streamed down his dusty cheeks as he slumped to the hay and sobbed. Micah had never allowed tears to flow so easily or so fully. He stopped suddenly, however, when he heard the sounds of three wagons rolling up the lane headed for the farm. "Who could that be?" he wondered as he wiped his tears on the back of his dirty gloved hand.

The cold air stung his face as he left the warmth of the barn and greeted the driver of the first wagon. "May I help you?"

"Could you direct us to the Millers' Farm?"

"I am Micah Miller and this is our farm."

He heard a gasp. "You cannot be serious!" In the second wagon sat the most beautiful girl Micah had ever seen, dressed in a fur-lined, indigo blue wool cloak. Her stern brown eyes with gold specks were the color of maple syrup; her golden brown hair had streaks of auburn.

James and Sarah briskly walked from the front door and approached the wagons. The young woman questioned, "Are you really Sarah Miller, the Sarah Bradford Miller who grew up in Weymouth?"

"Indeed I am," she turned to James in confusion. Just then Benjamin and Ethan arrived upon the scene.

"Well," she attempted to regain her composure, "I do hope you were not sick with worry over me. I am nearly three weeks overdue. I must tell you this entire journey from Boston has been a most unpleasant ordeal."

"Grace Alden Peabody?!" The older Millers responded in unison.

"Of course. Who else were you expecting?" She demanded. Suddenly she turned pale and her voice began to quake. "Did you not receive my grandfather's letter? Did you not know that I was coming to live with you?"

Sarah opened up her arms as James helped Grace down from the wagon. "Grace, our home is your home. You do not ever need an invitation," she hugged her warmly. "You must be exhausted, you poor thing. Come on in out of the cold while the men carry in your things."

James noticed a look of disdain as Grace glanced around their modest home. The 16-foot-square great room was where the family lived. The large fieldstone hearth was in the center of the back wall flanked on one side with the pine cupboard and shelves brimming with crockery, plates, cups and cooking utensils and the other with Sarah's spinning wheels. The left wall with its two small windows had a bench and a small bookcase. The massive Liberty Table took up nearly the entire center of the room. To the right was James' and Sarah's bedroom and next to that was Abigail's small room. A ladder led to the sleeping loft where the three brothers slept.

"Gentleman, do be careful with that," Grace instructed James and Micah as they carried in the tall clock and gingerly placed it in the corner along the front wall. "Those four trunks contain my personal belongings, you may put them in my closet for now," she motioned to Ethan and Benjamin. Apparently she had mistaken Abigail's bedroom to be her closet. "Mrs. Miller, these four chests are for you. There is tea -"

"From China?" Benjamin interrupted.

"Of course it is from China. Where else does tea come from?" she snapped in exasperation. "Then there's spices, sugar and other trifles. Some table linens, tea sets, draperies.

Grandfather insisted that I bring some practical items. I do not wish to be a burden. But I am only here until the war ends and Papa comes for me."

There was a moment of uncomfortable silence. Outside, Ethan and Benjamin were unable to slide one particularly heavy trunk off the wagon. "What do you have in here, rocks?" Ethan grumbled.

"Books. I wanted to keep some of Papa's favorite books safe with me. He would be terribly disappointed if anything happened to them while I was away."

"What kind of books?" Benjamin asked curiously.

"Papa has eclectic tastes in reading," she vaguely responded.

James and Micah hopped up onto the back of the wagon, and with some difficulty managed to carry the trunk into the house and slide it under the far end of the Liberty Table. "It's out of the way, safe and dry and it can double as a bench when company calls," James explained in his practical manner.

"Whoa! What kind of desk is this?" Ethan called from the last wagon.

"Be careful, young man. That desk and armoire are Chippendales."[2]

Ethan had no idea what chips and dales were.

It took fully an hour for the wagons to be unloaded and the house to be crammed with furniture and trunks piled upon each other.

"Thank goodness, you did not bring a four poster bed, or you would have to sleep in the barn," James joked.

"It is coming with the second shipment. I could not fit everything in one trip. I must tell you I have no intentions of ever sleeping in a barn."

"Grace, dear, Mr. Miller was merely teasing. When we get you unpacked and settled everything will fall into place. Ethan, please set the table."

"I know supper will not be fancy," she apologized. "We have plenty of roast pork, cornbread, butter, applesauce, squash and corn to fill up my four hungry farm boys. " As the family took their seats, James pulled out Abigail's chair next to Sarah's for Grace to sit.

James sat at the head of the table, Sarah to his right with her back to the hearth. Benjamin took his seat directly across Grace with Ethan to his left. "Where is Micah?" James asked as he glanced at the empty space to his left.

"Coming, Sir," he called from the loft as he headed down the ladder.

"Are you going to church?" Ethan asked his oldest brother who was now scrubbed clean and wearing his best linen shirt and brown wool britches.

Micah blushed. James cleared his throat and gave Ethan a stern look. The family bowed their heads. "Almighty God, we thank Thee for your protection and for delivering Grace safely to our home. We thank Thee for your ample provisions and help us to always be thankful for all the many blessings Thou hast bestowed upon us. Amen."

Half way through the meal, Grace asked Sarah, "Where is your daughter? Grandfather thought I would be a refining influence upon her."

Sarah dropped her fork and struggled to hold back tears from her panic-frozen eyes. "Grace, dear. Please excuse me. I have not been well lately and I fear all of this excitement has done me in. I need to rest. Tomorrow is a new day and we shall begin to unpack." She slowly stood up and went to her room.

"How dare she?" Benjamin silently fumed. "A refining influence indeed!" Ethan continued eating as Micah shyly gazed across the table.

It was James who finally spoke. "Grace, Mrs. Miller and our daughter, Abigail were both seriously ill. My wife is still recovering and tires easily. Unfortunately, Abigail died three months ago and the family is still grieving."

Grace blushed crimson and brought her finger tips to her mouth. She quickly regained her composure, "Good sir, I do beg your forgiveness…"

"You had no way of knowing," Micah consoled in his most grown-up voice. "Letters travel very slowly. That is why we did not know about your arrival. We are very sorry for your loss as well."

"You are very kind, Michael. Events unfolded rather quickly. After my mother's death Grandfather decided I was to live with your family. I promise I will not be a financial burden. Grandfather will see to that. It is only temporary until Papa can come for me."

"Grace, you have already been more than generous," James smiled warmly. "Your mother was a dear friend to Mrs. Miller and you shall be part of our family for as long as circumstances prescribe."

"Thank you, sir. If you gentleman will excuse me, I think I shall retire early as well. It has been a long and vexing day."

Micah stood up like a gentleman when she arose from her seat. Ethan continued eating while Benjamin stared into the fire and bit his lip.

"This has certainly been an interesting day," James tried to sound cheerful. "Boys, we shall clean up and also go to bed early. We have a long, busy day tomorrow if we hope to have that frame ready for raising in six weeks.

Within the hour, the brothers were climbing the ladder to the sleeping loft. Three narrow beds covered with wool blankets and quilts were lined up in a row. Each boy had a pine chest at the foot of his bed. One small table between Micah's and Ethan's bed held a candle. Benjamin's bed was cozily tucked under the eaves with a narrow bookcase which contained his favorite books and a candle. The boys hung their clothing on pegs.

Benjamin hissed, "What an arrogant, pompous-"

"Shhhh! She will hear you," Micah warned.

"Grandfather, thought I might be a refining influence," Benjamin imitated.

"Enough!" Micah whispered. "Where is your compassion? She recently lost both her parents; she had to leave her home to come live with strangers who were not even expecting her. How would you feel?"

Benjamin and Ethan hated when Micah tried to act grownup. They hated it even more when he was right.

"Look at the bright side. Maybe she will do the dishes and feed the chickens," Ethan suggested hopefully.

"No one will ever take Abigail's place. You know that." Micah consoled. "It will be an adjustment for all of us."

Benjamin blew out his candle without responding. As he lay there silently staring into the darkness, he began to wonder about the books in the trunk.

Benjamin was actually thankful to be spending the entire morning in the barn with his brothers and father. The brothers had risen, had done their morning chores, had eaten breakfast and headed to the barn before Grace had awakened. He knew he could not hide in the barn forever; he would need to return to the house. However, for now it was his sanctuary.

To be truthful, he enjoyed his new status as "chief architect". 'Measure twice, cut once," James reiterated. "Benjamin, double check these figures, please. Benjamin, take a second look at this diagram. "

He learned he enjoyed the smell of cut pine; and he was not half bad at joinery; he appreciated Ethan's new-found respect and in return he discovered his younger brother was quite talented.

Ethan could no longer stand the gnawing hunger in his growling stomach. "It is past noon."

James looked up at the sun. "That is true enough. It has been a productive morning. We will take a break for dinner."

As the four of them approached the back door, they heard peals of laughter. James smiled broadly for it was good to hear Sarah laughing again.

"Mercy! Don't tell me it's already dinner time!" Sarah put down her tea cup. The boys looked around the room in astonishment. Everywhere they looked were opened trunks filled with silk stockings, garters, under-petticoats, ribbons, hoop petticoats, stomachers, linen petticoats, stays, lace neckerchiefs, shifts, silk petticoats, silk hats, linen hats, straw hats in every color of the rainbow, skirts, gowns, cloaks, shawls, lace and leather shoes, silk shoes, and linens shoes with buckles and bows. Lying across the table was a gold brocade gown with pearls sewn on the front bodice.[3]

"Grace, dear, do tell the story about this dress."

"Well, I must have been five or six years old when Mrs. Adams came to visit with Nabby, John Quincy and Charles. Nabby, John and I escaped up to my parents' room to play dress up. My mother always said that John Quincy was the most compliant child she ever met and I should be more like him. Well, Nabby convinced him to put on this gold brocade dress, my mother's favorite, and we dressed up as well. We were giggling and carrying on and we did not hear our mothers coming up the stairs. Then in sweeps Mrs. Adams, "John Quincy, what would your father say! Although, gold brocade does become you."

Sarah and Grace once again laughed, although the boys did not find any humor in the situation. "Papa says John Quincy will go far in life and the two of us make a good match. I shall wear this dress when the two of us get married," she announced.

"Not if he wears it first," Benjamin growled. Sarah and Grace laughed even harder. Was he doomed to spend the rest of his life listening to the exploits and adventures of John Quincy Adams?

Dinner was an unsatisfactory affair for the brothers. It went by too quickly for Micah, too slowly for Benjamin, and in Ethan's opinion there was not enough food. However, a smiling James gratefully listened to Sarah and Grace's easy banter and laughter.

As father and sons headed back to the barn, James spotted Limbo admiring the timber frame. "Limbo, my friend," James greeted the African. "Did you come to see the timber frame?"

"Yes, sir. Mr. Osgood and I plan to come for the barn raising."

"We will need you! It is a big frame and we will need all the help we can get."

"Mr. Benjamin, how are you feeling? I have missed you this winter."

Limbo, who was born in Guinea, was kidnapped on the African coast, sold into slavery and brought across the Atlantic in a slave ship. No one knew the details of his early life. He was once the slave of a man named William McClellan in Gorham before escaping to Pequawket to his freedom. The Millers never heard the story of how Limbo became the slave of Mr. Moses Ames, one of the original settlers. They did know that because Mr. Ames treated him unkindly, Samuel Osgood offered to buy him.[4]

Before Abigail and Sarah became ill, Benjamin had been teaching the forty-three year old slave to read and write. His goal was to read the "Good Book" for himself. Limbo was very proud when Abigail gave him her old slate, a much used Blue Book Speller in a black wool bag with "Limbo" lovingly embroidered on the front.

"Did you stop by for a reading lesson? I think we can spare Benjamin for a half hour," James offered.

Suddenly Limbo's eyes filled with tears. "I sure do miss my little Miss Abigail."

"We all do," James sighed.

"Mr. Miller, I prayed day and night for the Good Lord to save her and she died anyway. I just do not see the use in praying no more."

Benjamin harbored these same sentiments. However he would never dare to express them to his father.

"Why do the righteous suffer? That's a question as old as the book of Job," James sadly smiled. Suddenly he felt very tired.

"Miss Abigail taught me all about Job, Mr. Miller. He was a man who was blameless and feared God who lived in Bible times. He had a wife and many children. He had 7000 sheep. I can't imagine taking care of 7000 sheep can you? Miss Abigail said a dozen sheep is a handful. He had 3000 camels. I have never seen a camel, have you? Miss Abigail said camels live in deserts and wouldn't want to live in Fryeburg because of the winter. He had 500 yoke of oxen and donkeys. Then one day the Devil took all that away from him to see if Job would still love God. Then the Devil made poor Job sick."

"Remember Satan could not do anything without the Lord allowing it," James added.

"You mean to tell me that the Lord allowed Miss Abigail to die?"

The brothers turned to their father eager to hear his response. They had silently asked themselves that very same question hundreds of times."

James sat down wearily. "The LORD giveth, and the LORD hath taken away; blessed be the name of the LORD," he quoted Job Chapter 1 verse 21. "Who are we to question the ways of the Almighty, the Creator of Heaven and Earth? We do not pray so the Lord will do what we ask. We pray that we will do what He asks us. It is not the number of years one spends upon this earth that matters. The important thing to remember is Abigail lives on in eternity with her Savior."

"Just does not seem right to me. If Abigail is spending eternity with the Good Lord - He could have let her spend a few more years with us."

"We live in a fallen world, my friend. In this world there is pain and sickness and death -"

"And slavery," Benjamin added.

"And slavery. I think God especially hates slavery because the Israelites were slaves to the Egyptians at one time."

"I know that. Miss Abigail told me all about Moses and the plagues, the parting of the Red Sea and the Promise Land. But how come if God hates slavery, why are there still slaves? Does God care about us?"

"The ground is perfectly level at the foot of the cross," James answered.

"Father means Jesus loves black people and white people equally," Benjamin explained.

"I know that. Miss Abigail already told me that. Why are you fighting the British for liberty? You white folks are already free. Why is Mr. Osgood's son James fighting at Falmouth? He is already free."

"I cannot answer all your questions. You are a wise man, my friend. But I can tell you that the Good Lord has a purpose for your life. Remember the story of Joseph?"

"Do you mean the 'Mary and Joseph' Joseph or the Joseph with the coat of many colors?"

"Joseph, the favorite son of Jacob; who had a coat of many colors. His other brothers were so jealous that they sold him into slavery."

"I remember. He ended up being a very important person in Egypt. When there was a famine, Joseph's brothers went to him for food."

"That's right, Limbo. God used a man who had been a slave to later save his family. God has a purpose for your life too. Now you and Benjamin go sit in that corner to study. We have work to do."

The next three days were exasperating for Benjamin. Grace held both Mother's and Micah's undivided attention. He was weary of her endless chatter, "Back in Boston we.... John Quincy said... Papa bought me the most beautiful.... When we were having tea at the Hancock's...." Father smiled at all her stories as if he actually enjoyed having her around! Grace sat in Abigail's seat and slept in her bed. Last night she picked up Abigail's carding combs as Sarah instructed her on the intricacies of carding fleece. No one mentioned Abigail anymore. It was as if she had never existed.

Benjamin entered the barn to feed and water the sheep. "What is wrong, Ebony? Are you not hungry?" He patted her black wooly head. "I know how you feel. I miss her too." He put his arms around her neck and pressed his cheek against her head.

"Benjamin, you are a very strange young man." Grace chided as she and Micah entered the barn.

Micah intervened. "Ebony is Abigail's prize sheep and pet. She raised it from a lamb after its mother died. Ebony is not eating much. I think she misses Abigail."

Grace looked at him raising one eyebrow.

"Animals have feelings too, you know. Abigail always hugged and talked to her sheep. Benjamin has taken over Abigail's chores and he is just trying to do what Abigail would have done," he defended his younger brother's behavior.

Ebony walked over toward Grace and stuck her nose through the fence to be patted. "I think she likes you. She wants you to pat her."

"I must tell you I am not touching that smelly animal," she turned away with her petticoats making a swishing sound. "What beautiful wood!" she admired the pieces of the timber frame lying on the floor. Are you building an addition to your house?"

"No, that is an addition to our barn."

"Why? Why would your dirty animals have a bigger and nicer home than the family?"

Benjamin was tempted to push her into the sheep pen and leave her there. Micah very calmly responded, "What is larger your father's ships or your house."

"The ships, naturally."

"Why?"

"Because that is the means by which he earns his living."

"Exactly," Micah continued. "This barn is a business investment. The expansion of the barn results in an expansion of our business."

"I understand the point which you are attempting to make. However, my father saw to it, that his family was properly cared for before he reinvested his wealth to expand his business."

"Your father was a smuggler and a slave trader!" Benjamin exploded.

"Benjamin!" Micah chastised.

"Michael, I do not need some farmer boy to defend me or my family!" she angrily turned to Micah. "My father is a successful and highly respected business man! We Peabodys have never owned a slave. We only have quality people in our employ."

"But you build the slave ships! Your grandfather could have built the ship that brought Limbo into slavery."

"Benjamin calm down. If I sold Socrates," Micah nodded his head toward the stallion," to a neighbor, and he in turn used Socrates to break into someone's barn and steal, I cannot be held responsible."

"That is a very flawed analogy," Grace contradicted. "Robbery is a crime. The slave trade is perfectly legal."

"It might be legal, but it is certainly immoral!" Benjamin answered.

"Well tell that to George Washington and Thomas Jefferson. They have slaves and I do not." With self-righteous indignation, she turned with a swish, picked her skirts up above her ankles and headed down the lane away from the house, toward the river. Micah watched her walk away.

"She does not need some farm boy to defend her," Benjamin mocked. "You are making a fool out of yourself. You will never be good enough for her. You are no John Quincy Ad-"

Benjamin never saw Micah's fist coming. However, James did. "Micah Bradford Miller!" he yelled just as his eldest son punched frail Benjamin in the chest sending him sprawling in the snow.

"I am sorry! I am sorry!" Micah knelt in the snow beside his brother who was gasping for breath and seeing black spots before his eyes. "I am so sorry!"

James came running. "Are you alright, son? Can you get up?"

Slightly dazed, he stood up with his father's assistance.

"Micah, there are times in a man's life, when he may be forced to fight—to defend his family, to protect his property. But a man never strikes someone out of anger—no matter how exasperating that person may be," he turned to Benjamin. "A man controls his anger. His anger does not control him."

"Now everyone go to the house. Let us give Miss Peabody a few moments of privacy and peace and quiet."

No one saw Grace as she tentatively reentered the barn. Lifting her skirts she cautiously walked towards the sheep pen. Eleven sheep - nine white and two black were milling around. Ebony stood all alone off to the far end of the sheep pen. She lifted her ears and turned her head toward Grace as she approached. The ewe stood on her hind legs, put her two front hooves on the fence, and tilted her head as if to say, "Well, what are you waiting for? Are you coming over?"

She timidly patted Ebony's soft, wooly head. "I am sorry you lost your mistress." she whispered as she handed her a handful of hay. "You are hungry." She kept whispering as she continued to hand over the hay. "Well, Abigail must have been a very special young lady, for everyone misses her so. If I died, who would miss me?

Grandfather says I am a beautiful, useless creature like my mother. Father was never home. Mother preferred her social life to me. Mrs. Adams has her hands full. The Millers certainly do not want me here."

"Grace, I have been looking all over for you," Micah was out of breath as he entered the barn.

"Whatever for?"

"It is getting dark and I was getting concerned that you might be lost or injured -"

"I am no concern of yours. Michael."

"It is Micah, not Michael. My name is Micah," he corrected. "And you are a concern of mine." He nodded at Ebony and smiled, "I see you made a new friend."

Grace looked up into his blue eyes and smiled coyly, "Yes, I believe I have."

VI

The Lord's Day

I t was the first Sunday the entire family would attend
church together since the onset of Abigail's illness.
Chores were quickly done, a breakfast hastily eaten and the
family dressed for church.

"Why are you wearing one of Father's waist coats and
frock coat?" Ethan asked his eldest brother. Benjamin was
tempted to say Micah was trying to dress like John Quincy
Adams, but kept silent.

"Because they no longer fit Father and they fit me now."
He tried to sound nonchalant.

Sarah looked thin and frail in her brown woolen dress
with the white collar and cuffs. Micah thought Grace looked
like a queen dressed in pale blue silk with matching shoes
and hat. She took her indigo blue cloak off the peg by the
door and Micah helped her put it on.

Ethan had hitched Aristotle and Socrates to the wagon
which was waiting in the lane. James helped Sarah up onto
her seat by his side. Micah lifted Grace up into the back
of the wagon where he had place several blankets over the
bench to provide cushion and warmth.

Grace had learned in order to be successful in business
and society one must refine one's powers of observation.

She quietly took in the surrounding countryside. There were no cobblestone streets, no brick homes, no obvious signs of wealth and prosperity. The passing landscape consisted of snow-blanketed fields, forests, the White Mountains to the west and one lone hill to the south with an occasional farmhouse and barn. Yet there was something tranquil about the pristine beauty of the countryside.

She quickly surmised wealth was not measured in pounds sterling but in acres of farmland and timber. Success was not measured by the number of your possessions, but by the size of your barn.

Back in Boston she had enjoyed attending services at North Church, an elegant brick building with white spires built in 1723. She admired the highly polished brass chandeliers imported from England. This Anglican Church, with strong ties to the British Crown, had been filled with Boston's members of the royal government, wealthy ship owners and merchants. Being members of the Church of England also set them apart from the majority of Boston's population who were Congregationalist.

Church members purchased their family pews. Prices for pews varied with the desirability of location. The Royal Governor and family had had their box pew right at the front of the church before he was forced to leave Boston back in 1776 with hundreds of government officials and Loyalists.[1] The Peabodys had their pew two rows directly behind them.

Grace was sorely disappointed when they arrived at "church". "My, this does not even look like a church," the disapproval was evident in her voice.

"Well, it is not," Micah explained. "Three years ago the town voted to construct a meeting house and raised 100 pounds for its construction. Isaac Abbot sold them an acre of land where we built a very nice 54 by 42 foot meetinghouse." Micah was proud that although he was only fourteen at the time, he had helped the men build it. "But the building is unheated so during the winter the town pays Isaac Abbott to heat a large room here at his house on Sundays."[2]

Grace noted that most families, like the Millers, arrived in unfashionable wagons. An elderly couple approached their wagon as James helped Sarah down.

"Sarah, dear," Mehitabel Frye took both of Sarah's hands into hers. "You have been in my prayers. I lost my first three children back in 1738.[3] A mother never gets over something like that. But we must learn to carry on for the sake of our families."

General Frye warmly shook James' hand. "It's good to have all of you back with us this Sunday." A veteran of the French and Indian War, Joseph Frye was called to Cambridge by General Washington at the outbreak of this war to assemble and organize recruits. He was promoted to Major General and was stationed at Falmouth. The following year he resigned his post and returned to Fryeburg claiming he was ill suited for active duty because of his age. However, Grace had already heard gossip that he resigned because he had serious differences with General Washington.[4]

"Mrs. Miller, it is so good to have you back with us," Mrs. Timothy Walker greeted Sarah. The Walkers were a prominent family in Fryeburg. Captain Timothy Walker built a mill at the outlet of Walker Pond. Ezekiel Walker was the first tavern keeper. Lt. John Walker was well known for his extraordinary size and strength.[5]

Sarah was greeted with words of sympathy, smiles and a few tears among the women. Grace was touched by the sincerity and concern the ladies displayed. No such displays of warmth and love were evident at her mother's funeral.

Clearly Mr. Frye was the "John Hancock" of the town. However, it was evident that Mr. Miller was highly respected by the other men—not for his possessions, but for his moral character. Ethan jumped off the wagon and joined some of the boys close to his age. After Micah helped Grace down from the wagon, he was soon surrounded by girls and young ladies with admiring glances.

Grace smiled politely as Micah introduced her to several of the town's people. Benjamin quietly, unnoticed, headed up the hill toward the house and waited by the door for the rest of the family to join him.

As the family entered, it bothered Grace that it appeared that people simply sat wherever they pleased. "Where is the family's pew?" she whispered to Micah.

"There is none."

"How do you know where to sit?"

"Father says we should let the older folks sit closest to the fire. We find a bench where we can sit together. It does not matter where," he quietly explained.

James Miller was a humble man who took the verse in Luke 14:11 seriously. "For whosoever exalteth himself shall be abased; and he that humbleth himself shall be exalted." He quietly led the family to an available bench in the last row.

After Grace recovered from her initial dismay, she realized the advantage from her seat. She was free to observe everyone without being observed herself.

It was obvious that the thirty-four year old minister, Reverend William Fessenden, was highly respected and admired by his congregation for he "preached the Gospel with fidelity, was filled with piety, well-educated and zealous to do good." He graduated from Harvard College and settled in Fryeburg in 1775.[6] He loved his Lord and his "flock".

As he stood up in front of his congregation, his eyes met Sarah's from the back row. His warm smile and the joy in his expression were evident even to Grace. He had always respected the Millers—James for his spiritual maturity and wisdom: Sarah for her warmth and hospitality; and each of the children who were uniquely talented.

Over the last six difficult months he had learned to love them. He had spent many hours by Abigail's and Sarah's bedside. During the last few days of Abigail's life he recited the 23rd Psalm many times. "The LORD is my shepherd, I shall not want." Just as Abigail had devoted her young life caring, loving and protecting her sheep, she had a Shepherd who would care, love and protect her for eternity.

Grace did not listen to the sermon. As a very young child, how many times did she hear Grandfather Alden tell her "all are sinners and have fallen short of the glory of God"? Unlike Grandfather Peabody, Grandfather Alden took his faith a little too seriously. That was to be expected since he was a direct descendant of Pilgrims John and Priscilla Alden. He was aghast when his daughter Elizabeth had joined the Anglican Church. Their family fled England in 1620 to escape the dictates of the Church of England. How could she turn around and join them! After that discussion, the Aldens were no longer invited to visit the Peabody mansion.

Grace spent the next two hours trying to figure out who the townspeople were. She had briefly met Mr. and Mrs. Samuel Osgood whose son Lt. James Osgood was stationed in Falmouth. She was not sure how Henry Osgood was related to them. However, she did know that he was a Harvard graduate. Dr. Joseph Emery, another Harvard graduate, was not there. Perhaps he was visiting a sick patient. There were the Merrills, the Clements, the Ames, the Evans, the Pages, and the Dressers. Would she ever keep everyone straight?[7]

Finally, when Grace thought she could no longer bear another minute sitting on that wooden bench, the sermon mercifully came to a conclusion. Of course Ethan was starving. James was concerned because Sarah looked exhausted and he quietly but briskly led the family out the back door and into their wagon.

"Until today, I never realized that there were so many shades of brown," Grace casually announced.

"It is the beginning of mud season," Micah explained. In a few months you will be amazed by all the various shades of green!"

"I meant," She corrected, "I have never seen so many shades of brown clothing." Truly Grace had been an island of brilliant blue in a drab sea of browns.

"Because of the war families here have to spin and weave their own flax and wool and make their own clothing. The climate here is much too cold to grow indigo. We can only use locally grown plants for our dye," Micah patiently explained.

"Really, Micah, do you not think I know that? I am a Peabody. The earliest mention of indigo is found in manuscripts from India dating back to the 4th century B.C. Marco Polo described the Indian indigo industry in his writings. In the 11th Century Arab traders introduced indigo to the Mediterranean area. It was not until Portuguese explorer Vasco de Gama discovered the sea route to India, when indigo was used in Europe after arriving through ports in Portugal, Spain, England and Holland. The Spanish had indigo plantations in South America.

The colony of South Carolina grows rice in the marshy areas and indigo plants on the high dry ground. They imported the seeds from Antigua and produced over a million pounds annually from 1745 -1775. Their exports have decreased dramatically since the outbreak of the war. Indigo is color-fast and should never be confused with the shade of blue from cheap blue dye from the woad plant"[8]

"The Greek word for dye is indikon," Benjamin interrupted.

"Yes, and in Latin the word is indicum which leads to our English word indigo," she concluded.

Benjamin looked at Grace in amazed disbelief.

"It is not every day that someone in petticoats proves to be more knowledgeable than you," Micah teased his brother.

"We Peabodys had an office in Charleston until the outbreak of the war. When it was no longer financially advantageous to keep it open, we concentrated our business endeavors in Philadelphia, New York and Boston. Grandfather oversees the Boston Office, Papa the one in Philadelphia and Papa's cousin Thomas the one in New York. Someday I will inherit the family business."

"What would your husband, John Quincy, think?" Benjamin challenged.

"He would think he was indeed a fortunate man to marry into such an esteemed family."

The brothers in the back of the wagon could not see their parents' amused smiles.

It was Sarah's custom to do the cooking for Sunday dinner on Saturday. To Grace's credit she did spend the entire day by Sarah's side, peeling and chopping vegetables as Sarah expertly maintained the fire on the left hand side of the hearth and shoveled small piles of burning coals on the right.

"Mrs. Miller, why are you doing that?" Grace asked curiously.

"Watch and you shall see. Would you like to make a pot of tea? Fill this teapot with water from the pitcher and then add your tea."

Grace took her pewter tea ball and carefully filled it with leaves of black tea. Sarah's teapot was a sturdy and fireproof earthen vessel, not like Grace's delicate porcelain one imported from China or the sterling silver one crafted by Paul Revere. With a long wrought iron hook, Sarah deftly placed an iron trivet on the coals and placed the teapot on the trivet.

"Fill this pot half way with water." Sarah placed a long S shaped hook onto the crane, placed the black cast iron pot onto the hook, and swung the crane over the fire. "When the water boils, we shall add the chopped butternut squash and dried corn kernels."

A pork roast had been impaled on a spit and placed into the tin kitchen hours ago and continued to slowly roast. "We cannot begin the cornbread until we have some buttermilk. Micah left a small bucket of cream on the back steps for us. Please bring it in."

"This was my mother's" Sarah explained as she placed on the table a small salt glazed butter churn approximately one foot tall. "Please begin churning while I fry four strips of bacon."

"Why do you need bacon for cornbread?"

"When you taste it, you shall know," Sarah smiled as she placed the bacon into the hanging griddle, swung the arm of the crane away from the fire, hooked the griddle unto another S shaped hook and swung the arm back over the fire.

Just when Grace was ready to complain that her right arm was getting tired Sarah spoke up," The butter should be done by now." She pulled off the cover. "Good job, Grace, and perfect timing. The bacon is ready and the bacon fat has cooled. Pour the buttermilk into this pitcher and place the butter in this wooden bowl for now."

Sarah quickly turned to the hearth, with a hook swung the crane over to her and announced, "The water has boiled. Place the squash and dried corn in here and swing the crane back over the fire."

Grace was so busy churning the butter she had forgotten about cooking the vegetables. "How did Mrs. Miller keep all these recipes and details straight?" she wondered as she gingerly placed the vegetables in the boiling water, picked up the long wrought iron hook and slowly swung the crane back over the flames. "Oh, what about the beans?"

"They have been cooked. We shall add them later."

Sarah placed a mixing bowl on the table. "Pour a cup of buttermilk into this bowl, she instructed, "and add 1 and ½ cups of cornmeal, one teaspoon of baking soda and one teaspoon of salt. Stir well while I add some cooled grease and crumbled bacon. Very good, now grease this skillet and I will pour the batter in." With the iron hook, she expertly placed the skillet directly into the hot coals, placed the cover tightly on, and then added coals to the top of the cover.

"Why are you doing that?" Grace asked.

"Because in order for the cornbread to bake, you must have heat evenly distributed. Without the coals on top, the batter would burn on the bottom before the top had a chance to cook. Shall we have a cup of tea?"

That sounded heavenly to Grace who wished to sit down and rest.

"Please run to the barn and ask Micah to dig up some parsnips and invite them in for tea. They have been working hard in the barn feeding the livestock and cutting more braces of the frame since after breakfast I am sure they would like a break."

After leaving the warmth of the hearth, the cold air took her breath away. She wrapped the white mohair shawl tightly as she ran into the barn.

"Is it time for dinner?" Ethan asked hopefully.

"It is still morning. But you are all invited for tea. Micah, your mother asks that you pick some parsnips."

"Ebony has been waiting for your visit all morning," Micah smiled.

Benjamin rolled his eyes for he knew that Micah kept glancing at the back door all morning waiting for her to visit.

"Did you miss me, my friend?" Grace patted Ebony on the head and handed her handfuls of hay. She even petted some of the others who strolled over out of curiosity.

Benjamin fought back tears. Ebony was Abigail's favorite and now she acts as if Abigail never existed. He angrily left the barn and helped Micah dig up parsnips.

Sarah always used only one end of the Liberty Table for meal preparation reserving the other end for dining. She had set the table with some of Grace's porcelain tea cups, put some of Grace's white sugar in the matching sugar bowl, laid out some linen napkins with pewter spoons. She had placed a few slices of yesterday's cornbread in a plate.

James looked around approvingly, "My, this does look special."

Sarah smiled. "Grace has been helping me in the kitchen and I finally have some energy to explore the items in the trunks. Gentlemen, please do not dawdle if you wish your dinner to be on time," she teased.

Grace barely finished her second cup of tea when Sarah exclaimed, "Mercy! We forgot to wash the butter."

"I did not know the butter was dirty."

James could hear Sarah's peals of laughter as he headed back to the barn and smiled.

"We need to wash off any buttermilk that may be still clinging to the butter. Any drops of buttermilk will soon sour and that would ruin our butter. Pour a little water from the pitcher and pour it over the butter in the wooden bowl. Now with this wooden paddle, stroke the butter. See how the clear water is turning milky? Drain the liquid and pour some more water. Repeat this process until the remaining liquid is clear. I believe the vegetables are cooked. Very good, Grace."

Grace radiated with pride as Sarah drained the vegetables and placed them back into a mixing bowl. "Chop this onion while I boil more water in the pot. As Grace chopped and the water boiled, Sarah melted some butter in a small hanging griddle. "Add your onions into the griddle and stir until they're golden brown. I shall wash and scrub the parsnips and throw them in the pot.

"The onions are beginning to burn! Swing the crane toward you so the pan is away from the fire. Keep stirring. That is better. While the parsnips are boiling add the fried onions to the squash and corn, add two handfuls of cooked beans. Add two teaspoons of brown sugar, some more of that melted butter salt and pepper."

"Is it done?" Grace asked hopefully.

Sarah smiled. "Not yet. Pour the bowl into this Dutch oven." Sarah quickly shoveled another small pile of hot coals in the hearth, placed the Dutch oven into the coals and placed the lid upon it. She added more coals on the cover of the corn bread.

"You forgot to place the coals on top of the vegetables," Grace reminded.

"We do not need to. We are not baking the vegetables; we are merely heating them through. The pork looks done. Set the table please while I slice the meat. Carefully remove the cover to the cornbread. Take care not to spill the ashes on the bread. Now place the pot off to the side for the bread to cool. Very good, Grace. Now swing the crane over to you. Are the parsnips done?[9]

Grace was most thankful that all the cooking was done on Saturday as she and the family entered the house after church.

"Benjamin, you do not need to reheat our dinner today. Grace will help me. Help your brothers bring in some firewood and water. Dinner will be served soon.

Grace set the table with her mother's best linen table cloth, china, silverware and glasses as Sarah placed the pot of vegetables in the coals to reheat, put the leftover parsnips in the griddle to fry in bacon drippings, reheated slices of cooked pork and placed her teapot on the trivet on the coals.

Grace placed slices of the best cornbread she ever tasted on the table with a dish of "her" butter and a bowl of applesauce. All the food was on the table waiting by the time the men returned to the house. The house was aglow with candle light as Grace placed two pewter candelabras on the table, one on the mantel and the fourth on a book case.

"Sarah!" James gasped. "Everything is beautiful— including you." She blushed and smiled. Benjamin was right. Sarah Bradford was born to be a lady, not a poor farmer's wife.

"It is the same old food. Grace set the table with her mother's things."

"Sarah, you are well enough to come to church, to prepare this wonderful meal, and to join us at the table. It has not been the same without you. We have much to thank the Almighty, for today has indeed been a special day."

The family stood in front of their seats as James asked the blessing. "Our Heavenly Father, we thank Thee for the freedom to worship in Your House and worship Thee in the way we see fit. We thank Thee for Sarah's growing strength and renewed health. We thank Thee for providing us with this bountiful meal and pray that Thou would bless the hands of those who have prepared it. We thank Thee for our three healthy sons and for bringing Grace to us who has added such joy to our lives. We thank Thee also for the promise of spring."

Grace stiffened, swallowed hard and blinked back tears. Did Mr. Miller actually thank God for bringing her here? Both Sarah and Micah smiled at her warmly.

Benjamin remained silent as the family passed the plates of food to one another. "Was he supposed to thank God for letting his sister die and sending this spoiled rich girl to replace her? She should pack up her fancy clothes and dishes and return to Boston!"

Ethan hungrily piled the mixed vegetables on his plate. "Of all my favorite foods, the three sisters are my favorite of the favorites."

"I beg your pardon," Grace turned to him. Ethan could not respond because his mouth was full.

"The mixture of squash, corn and beans is called the three sisters by the Indians," Micah explained. "You see the Indians taught the settlers how to plant the squash, beans and corn together. The beans grow up along the corn stalks and the squash grows along the ground between the stalks. They grow well together and they taste good cooked together."[9]

"How interesting," Grace smiled and Micah blushed.

"Sarah, I have been thinking," James interrupted. "This house was just perfect for the three of us fifteen years ago. And it has continued to serve us well all these years. However, it is now clear to me that our once small family has rapidly outgrown it. Furthermore, the family will only grow larger as the boys grow up, marry and begin families of their own. I have therefore decided to use the timber frame as an addition to the house, rather than a barn. You know Grace's four poster bed will be arriving sometime soon, and she refuses to sleep in the barn," he grinned.

Micah and Ethan were ready to protest until they saw the joy on their mother's face.

"Oh, James, truly? That would be lovely! But what about your barn?"

"We have no shortage of trees. As soon as the house is done, the four of us will begin cutting a new frame for the barn. What does our resident architect think of that?" he turned to Benjamin.

Benjamin was intrigued with the notion of living in a much larger and grander house. Perhaps they could have a library, or his own bedroom. "The frame is large enough that we could build it right over the existing house. We might not interrupt Mother and Grace very much if we did it that way."

Grace interrupted excitedly, "Picture walking in the front door into a foyer with a grand staircase in front of you. To the left will be the drawing room with the Chippendale desk and tall clock."

"Yes, with the walls covered with book cases from floor to ceiling, and all completely filled with books!" Benjamin added.

"Only two walls of books," Grace corrected. "The west wall facing the river shall have large windows. The interior wall will need a fireplace."

"Across from the drawing room will be our bedroom. Large enough for a sitting area by the fireplace," Sarah continued excitedly. "Behind the drawing room will be the formal dining room. Behind the dining room will be this room—the kitchen—with a proper pantry!"

Grace continued, "Behind your bedroom, will be my bedroom with plenty of space for my four poster bed and armoire. What will be behind my bedroom?"

"A work room where mother can spin and weave and we can make baskets whittle and work on projects. This way we do not have to clean up and put everything away every time it's time to eat," Ethan piped up.

"Could the three of us have our own bedrooms upstairs," Micah asked hopefully.

"Of course! Plus a guest room and a back staircase as well," Sarah beamed.

"Whoa! Whoa! The four of us cannot get this all done before planting!" James interjected. "You know the plan for the barn was to get the frame up and the roof on this spring. After harvest, we will work on enclosing it. During the winter we would begin the interior work."

"With all due respect, sir, I must tell you a handful of farmers cannot possibly build as grand a house as this shall be. Do you not agree that this is a job for master carpenters? I shall write to grandfather and have him send us his best workers for the summer. I am sure Ethan would love to work with them."

"Could we, Father?" Ethan asked excitedly.

"Son, you know well that we have not the money to pay carpenters. We need to stop daydreaming and build this for ourselves. By the grace of God, and with his continued blessing, we Millers shall continue to provide for our own daily bread and also provide adequate nightly shelter."

"Sir, if you will provide all the raw materials, I will provide for the labor." Grace abruptly left the table, took a sharp knife from the cupboard, immodestly lifted her skirt to her knees and opened one seam of her petticoat. Out rolled three gold coins!

The family gasped as she placed the coins into James' hand. "Good sir," Grace smilingly explained, "I must tell you, I have plenty of petticoats!"

VII

The Promise of Spring

Word of the new house spread quickly in Fryeburg; spring arrived more slowly. Unexpectedly, James entered through the back door one midmorning as Grace was complaining about the weather.

"This is supposed to be spring? I must tell you I do not see any green grass growing, trees budding, flowers blooming or robins landing. All I see is mud, melting snow piles, more mud, puddles and more mud!"

"Cabin fever?" James asked as he sat down at the head of the table and took out an envelope. "Grace, I have been corresponding with your Grandfather. We never did receive his first letter to us—the one announcing your arrival—but I assured him that you had arrived safely, you have been most helpful in the kitchen and feeding the sheep, and asked about the availability of his master carpenters. I know you wrote to him first, but I am certain he wanted my approval before he sent out workers.

There have been some interesting recent events you may want to hear about. It appears that your father's cousin Thomas and his family will be arriving in Boston mid-September and they will be moving into your house."

"What!" Grace gasped. "Those people have no right to MY house. Grandfather has no right in letting those people live there. That house belongs to my father. He would never consent to such a thing!"

"Now Grace," James began calmly. "You know it is not good for a house to be left vacant. It encourages vandalism. What would your father think if he returned home after the war only to find his beloved house destroyed? Your grandfather was very prudent in finding new tenants. What better tenants than family who would take good care of it?"

Sarah continued, "I can only imagine how difficult it must be during war time for a family to find such elegant housing in Boston. What other house in Boston could meet the high standards and discriminating tastes of a Peabody family member?"

"In early September your grandfather will be loading *The Amazing Grace* with all the contents of your home and shipping it to Falmouth. We will have to make arrangements to bring the items back here by wagon.

Two master carpenters and fourteen of their assistants will arrive the beginning of June. I am making arrangements for them to be boarded with the Fryes, the Walkers, the Abbotts, the Osgoods and the Dressers. He stated that I am financially responsible to pay their wages. Apparently, he knows nothing about your golden petticoats, Grace. He wonders how such a young girl came into possession of such a large sum of money."

"Is he accusing me of stealing? How dare he!" she pounded her fist violently on the table.

"Perhaps you can defend your honor and explain how you came by that money."

"It was Papa's custom when he returned from a voyage to set aside some money for my mother in case an emergency arose in his absence. It was hidden in a small wooden box behind some bricks in the chimney of my parents' bedroom.

The war broke out when I was a little girl. He then began bringing home lots of coins for me as well. He instructed us that if we had to leave our house in a hurry, we were to sew the coins in our petticoats, pack our clothes, leave everything else behind and flee.

When my mother died, I took her money and her petticoats as well as my own. Papa wants me to have this money. My grandfather knows nothing about this. That is the way Papa wants it to be. I choose to spend my money in building this house. Papa would call it a wise investment."

"Tonight when the boys are upstairs in bed, we will retrieve your coins, place them in some jars. We have a secret place under the boards under our bed where we store things. No one outside of this family is to hear about this," James warned. "That is your money to invest as you see fit. When it is time for you to leave, you will take the remainder with you. I will put that in writing -"

"The sap is running!" Ethan burst in upon them breathlessly.

"What does that mean?" Grace asked.

"It is sugaring time. Ethan's favorite time of year," James smiled at his eager son.

"You are joking with me again, Mr. Miller. Everyone knows sugar does not grow on trees."

"Not ON trees, IN trees," Ethan explained. "Let us gather up the buckets. We do not have a minute to lose," he ran out as quickly as he had run in.

"You heard the boss," James winked at Sarah. "We do not have a minute to loose. You know where to find me," He whistled as he headed toward the barn.

In the scurry of gathering buckets, spiles and barrels, no one heard Sarah as she entered the barn with tears in her eyes. "Sarah, Dear, what is wrong?" James put down an armful of buckets.

"There is a limit to what a woman can take," she sniffled.

"Of course there is," he put his arm lovingly around his wife. "I was afraid you were over doing. Get some rest and have Grace prepare dinner."

"I do not need rest. I need a moment of peace!" she burst into tears. "She is by my side every waking minute! Grace refuses to step out doors because she does not wish to get mud on her shoes, or her silk stockings, or her petticoat, or her cloak."

"Sarah, perhaps you should lend her some of Abigail's work clothes."

Benjamin was horrified. Sarah sobbed, "I could not stand to see someone else wearing Abigail's clothing!"

"It will be difficult for all of us. But if Abigail was with us, I am certain she would willingly share her work clothes so Grace could go outdoors and be with the rest of the family."

"Mother, this would only be temporary until the two of you have the opportunity to make some other clothes for her. Perhaps you have an old shift or apron she could borrow as well," Micah suggested. "I shall be happy to take her sugaring with me for the next few weeks."

"That is very generous of you, son," James tried not to smile. "I am sure your mother will greatly appreciate this."

Just as Hercules and Zeus were hitched to the wagon filled with buckets and barrels, Grace appeared apprehensively. "I must tell you I certainly do not look like a Peabody."

"No. You look more like a Miller," Micah smiled with approval.

"You look like a chickadee instead of a peacock," Ethan observed.

"That is an incorrect analogy. Everyone knows that the peacock is the male. The peahen is not colorful at all," Grace contradicted. That was exactly what Benjamin was going to say.

"That was meant to be a compliment, Grace," James grinned. "Sit up front with me."

Ten minutes later, James stopped the oxen in front of a grove of maples. Micah, you, Grace and Ethan start here. Benjamin and I will go further down."

"But we always do this together," Ethan contradicted.

"Well now you are mature enough to work with Micah without my supervision. Get your snowshoes on, grab some buckets. Micah, take his sack with the spiles, bit and brace and we will be back in a while."

"How do these things work?" Grace tried attaching her foot to a snowshoe.

"The snow is still too deep to walk on. I made these a couple of years ago. It redistributes your weight on a larger surface so you do not sink," Micah explained as he tightened the rawhide strap across her boot.

"You invented these? How ingenious!"

"Indians invented them a long time ago. He just copied them, that is all," Ethan explained. "Just like Indians invented maple syrup and maple sugar. Now follow me," he instructed as he picked up some buckets. Grace awkwardly followed with Micah offering words of encouragement.

At the first maple, Micah expertly drilled a hole with his bit and brace, inserted the spile and hooked a bucket on. Drip, drip, drip. He repeated the process on the other side on the same tree.

Grace discovered she enjoyed being a chickadee. She loved the freedom of movement that the absence of corsets, silk stockings and hoop skirts afforded. "I want to do this tree next!" she motioned.

"It is too small. If you can put your arms around a tree and just touch your fingertips, then you know it is the right size," Ethan explained.

Undaunted, she walked up to a huge tree where her arms barely reached halfway. "We can do this one!"

Ethan laughed so hard he dropped a bucket. "That is a pine tree you silly goose!"

"This looks like a good spot," offered James stopping the oxen a few yards before the Saco. "It sure is beautiful." Snow still covered the tops of the White Mountains while the snow-melt swelled the river with rushing white water. "This is where I come to pray and cry," he confided to his son.

Benjamin turned to his father in surprise. "Why are you so surprised? I miss her every minute of every day. To think I almost lost your mother and you as well!" he put his arm around his son and swallowed hard. "Do you not think I have not asked why? Why Abigail?" he slowly shook his head. "Sorrow is no sin. But do not become bitter, Benjamin. Abigail would not want us to. It is not Grace's fault her mother died and she ended up with us. Do not forget she is grieving too. Only she is grieving all alone. At least we have each other. When I look up at these mountains I think of the Psalmist, 'I will lift up mine eyes unto the hills, from whence cometh my help. My help cometh from the LORD, which made heaven and earth."

We will tap a few trees and head back. Your brother will be hungry for dinner." Father and son worked silently side by side. Sometimes words are not needed.

Ethan was not the only hungry child at dinner. Grace, with bright rosy cheeks and wind swept hair, declared herself "starving". After helping Sarah clean up after dinner, she ran out to the barn to check on the sheep and to chat with Ebony before climbing back into the wagon with the Millers. This time, the five of them stayed together and worked as a team dumping buckets of sap into the large barrels on the back of the wagon and replacing the buckets. Once home they had a bucket brigade as they emptied the barrels into a huge cast iron pot and lit a fire.

"Wow! Look at all that sap!" Grace admired.

"It is a lot, for it takes 40 gallons of sap to make one gallon of syrup. Then we boil down the syrup to make maple sugar." Micah explained.

"That is a lot of work just for sugar!"

"And building ships, sailing them to the Caribbean, hoping not to get captured by the British or boarded by pirates, buying cane sugar and hoping not to get caught by a hurricane on your way home is not a lot of work?" Benjamin contradicted.

"We Millers prefer to do things ourselves." Micah boasted.

It was well after ten o'clock that evening and Micah was still outside stirring the bubbling mixture. Grace, dressed in her peacock clothes, brought out some cornbread. "I thought you might be hungry," she offered.

"No, that would be Ethan. He has two hollow legs. But I do appreciate this. I thought you were afraid to get your clothes muddy."

"Your mother assured me that the ground was frozen. She also told me to bring out two mugs and two spoons."

Micah filled the mugs with clean snow and poured some maple syrup on it. Grace skeptically tried some. "This is so good! I have never had anything like this!"

"It is our annual treat. We must enjoy the maple syrup as much as we can now. Unfortunately the syrup will not keep and will get moldy. That is why we cook the syrup down to sugar."

"Do you not get lonely or bored out here?" she asked.

"I enjoy occasional solitude. I am certainly not bored. Look up."

Grace turned her face to the heavens and gasped, "Look at those stars!"

"The heavens declare the glory of God, and the firmament sheweth his handy work," he quoted Psalm 19:1. "That medium-bright star is Polaris, the North Star. It is part of the Little Dipper and there is the Big Dipper. See how the two stars on the dipper end point straight to Polaris? Look over there in the southern sky, that group of stars is called Orion the Hunter."

Every day that week Grace was outdoors snowshoeing through the woods, tapping trees, emptying buckets. Every evening she spent outdoors by Micah's side for her astronomy lesson. Every night she went to bed exhausted and fell asleep as soon as her head hit the pillow.

When the family returned home from church, Ethan complained, "I do not see why we cannot go this afternoon."

"You know very well it is Sunday. 'Thou shalt keep Holy the Sabbath'." James reminded.

"But the trees do not know what day it is!" Ethan argued.

"The trees may not, but we and the Lord certainly do."

After Sunday dinner, Grace put on her "chickadee" clothing and strolled down to the river. An only child accustomed to living in a spacious home, she often found the congeniality of the Millers to be overwhelming and longed for privacy.

"What if Papa never returns?" The questions plagued her at unexpected moments. She fought back tears. No, she had to have faith. Her mother promised her that he would return.

She did not hear Ethan stealthily approach her and hide behind a pine tree. Suddenly he jumped out yelling an Indian war whoop causing a shrieking Grace to stumble into the snow.

"You better be more careful, Grace," he warned. "You could get scalped. You know there was a big Indian battle just down the road. Now they are on the warpath! John Lovewell-"

Grace did not stay to hear the rest of the story as she picked up her skirts and ran toward the barn. "Mr. Miller! Mr. Miller, the Indians are after me!"

"What Indians?" James asked perplexed.

"The Indians from the big battle down the street. Ethan says..."

"Did Ethan frighten you about the battle between Captain John Lovewell and Paugas, the sachem of the Pequawket Tribe? Did he happen to mention that it happened way back in May of 1725? Any Indians you may happen upon today are peaceable."

James Miller was a sensitive man who believed that every human life was of value simply because mankind was created in the image of God. Unlike his youngest son and most men of Fryeburg he did not relish retelling the story of the Indian battle. "Captain Lovewell's hometown of Dunstable suffered from frequent Indian attacks. One day he raised a company of men and headed north to put an end to the attacks. Yes, there was a terrible battle at Saco Pond which we now call Lovewell Pond.[1] That was over fifty years ago. No Fryeburg citizen has been molested by an Indian that I know of.

However, in the future please inform Mrs. Miller or me if you intend to take a walk. It is easy to get lost in the woods."

That evening, Ethan Jacob Miller went to bed without his supper.

When breakfast and chores were finished Monday morning the five of them climbed the wagon and headed down the lane. James dropped off Micah, Ethan and Grace — for they planned to snowshoe up the hill and tap some new trees — and continued on with Benjamin.

"How come Benjamin always gets to be with Father?" Ethan whined.

"Because it is his season."

"What do you mean it is his season?" Grace inquired.

"Well, when the other children were much younger, I spent all of my time with Father, and he taught me everything I know about farming. The past two years Father spent a great deal of time with Ethan teaching him about woodworking, tools and trees. Now it is Benjamin's turn."

"What is your father teaching him?"

"To be a man."

Benjamin unexpectedly broke the silence. "It should have been me."

"What do you mean, it should have been you?" James asked as he continued down the lane.

"It should have been me who died. Mother needed Abigail, and Micah and Ethan work with you all the time. It would have been better if I had died instead of Abigail."

He stopped the oxen, then turned to his middle son and looked him in the eyes. "What would Abigail have done if you had died? You were always the stronger, healthier and braver of the two. If you are overwhelmed with grief, how do you think she would manage? You have been a great help and comfort to your mother these past few months. But I do not think your sister would have done half as well. It would have been as if your mother lost both her children. Please do not ever think that again."

"But Micah will take over the farm; Ethan will be the best carpenter in Fryeburg but I..."

"And you will be a famous lawyer like John Adams. Besides," James grinned, "John Adams is not the only one with a brilliant son. Do not tell your brothers I said that."

"I think they already know. Did you really go to Harvard with Mr. Adams? What was he like?"

"He was short, stocky and had no sense of humor. I do not know what Abigail sees in him. Do not tell your mother I said that."

For the first time in six months Benjamin laughed out loud.

The short maple syrup season was over. One morning after breakfast Sarah smiled, "Grace, I believe I am feeling up to having an adventure. Are there any more trunks for us to unpack?"

"The cook insisted that I bring this one with me," Grace explained as she opened the lid. "Oh, I remember seeing this. My mother called it the spice box. Its drawers are filled with dried leaves and beans."

The barn red, wooden box with nine drawers was a treasure chest to Sarah! The first drawer was filled with coffee beans. "Oh, Mr. Miller will be so delighted to have coffee with his breakfast tomorrow. We shall make is a surprise," she said with a twinkle in her eyes. The next two drawers held dried sage and mint. The second row of drawers held coriander, mustard seeds and mace. However, it was the bottom row that excited her the most. "Cinnamon sticks! I have not had cinnamon in years!" She then held up a handful of dried pits. "Could it be? Nutmeg from the Spice Islands!"[2]

"What do we do with these sticks and nuts?" Grace asked.

"We grate them with this tin grater and we add the powder to our cooking or baking. Hasty pudding shall be a treat with these." She opened the very last drawer. "Tapioca! The children never had tapioca."

"I found these things at the bottom of the trunk," Grace held up two loaves of white sugar wrapped in light blue paper[2]

"Tomorrow we shall celebrate with coffee, tapioca pudding with cinnamon and whipped cream!"

"What are we celebrating?" Grace asked as she surveyed the sugar and spices laid out on the Liberty Table.
"Our blessings!"

Grace knelt in the barn with wide-eyed amazement. "It is a miracle," she whispered to Micah as she watched another lamb being born.
"Micah smiled. "This is why I love being a farmer. Last week it was the piglets, this week the lambs. Every spring brings new life; every fall brings a new harvest. Every season has new challenges and responsibilities. I do not understand how Benjamin thinks farming is boring."
"When will the baby oxen be born?" she asked innocently.
Micah's laughter filled the barn. "Oxen do not have babies."
"I may not be a farm girl, but I do know how babies are made. Each species has a male and a female and-"
"There is no such thing as a female ox."
Grace put her hands on her hips. "Micah Miller, are you teasing me? If there is no such thing as female oxen, where do baby oxen come from?" she challenged.
"Oxen are castrated bulls."
Her mouth dropped open. "I must tell you that is so disgusting!" With a swish of her petticoats, she left the barn.

Both Reverend and Mrs. Fessenden had a gift for making anyone and everyone feel special. The pastor had great compassion for the thin, frail, grief-stricken Benjamin and often initiated conversations with him after church, or visited him at home. Mrs. Fessenden looked beyond Grace's silks, satins and petticoats. She saw a frightened, friendless, lonely child who was probably friendless and lonely back in Boston as well. Grace soon discovered under her rustic exterior that Mrs. Fessenden was an educated and refined lady. In mid-April, after the sap and mud had dried up, they went to visit the Millers for tea under the pretense of dropping off a meal and a book.

Grace, the perfect hostess, was preparing for this visit for days. She set the Liberty Table with her mother's linen table cloth and napkins, porcelain tea set, and silverware. Hoping to impress Mrs. Fessenden, Grace wore a beige open robe elaborately embroidered with flowers, revealing a white quilted petticoat. Her bodice and stomacher was made of matching beige silk. The ruffles at her neck and sleeves matched her petticoat.[3]

"That is a beautiful frame," the minister admired as he entered the Miller's barn.

"Will you be coming to the frame raising?" Benjamin asked.

"I do not know if I will be much help, but we will both be there."

Mrs. Fessenden knocked and entered the house through the back door. "Mrs. Miller, I know how very busy you have been of late, so I brought you a meal."

Grace looked at the watery soup and thought even the Peabody's servants ate better than this. Then she realized that perhaps this was the very best this good woman had to offer.

Sarah graciously thanked her guest for her thoughtfulness as Grace shoveled some coals to one side of the hearth and carefully placed the trivet. She filled her tea ball with tea and placed the teapot on the trivet.

Benjamin arrived through the back door with a bucket of water. "Father thought you might have need this. Oh, Grace-"

"Just put it down, Benjamin."

"But Grace!"

"Benjamin, I am busy!"

"Grace!"

The men could hear Grace's screams from the barn when Benjamin threw the bucket of water at her.

"Mercy!" Sarah exclaimed.

"You incorrigible child! I hate you Benjamin Miller," Grace screamed as James and Rev. Fessenden entered.

"What is the meaning of this, son?" James demanded.

"Grace, your petticoat was on fire."

VIII

The Raising

G race Peabody was an impatient, young woman who believed one should never work if one can hire someone else to do it for you. She insisted that it would take too much precious time if the Millers dug the foundation themselves. After all, are there not men who would willingly work for hard currency during the weeks before planting?

James Miller was a humble man who believed one should never hire someone for work he could do himself. Finally, after several discussions around the Liberty Table, it was James' tired and sore lower back that convinced him of the wisdom of Grace's proposal.

As soon as the frozen ground thawed, Grace placed an advertisement for laborers in the window of Mr. Frye's store:

Help Wanted
Laborers desiring of paid work are wanted to help dig and lay a large foundation. Must supply own shovel, pick and dinner. We will pay 2 shillings, 3 pence for a full day of work. Able-bodied men aged 16 years and older may report to the James Miller farm at dawn on April 4th of this year.

The number of men and boys who appeared that morning was more than she expected, for there were few men in Fryeburg unwilling to do honest, hard work for a few shillings. Because many of the men between the ages of eighteen and thirty were away at the War, most of her recruits were over the age of forty or younger teenage boys.

The first to arrive, carrying two shovels, was Limbo. "Mr. Osgood says he is too old for this kind of work and his son is still off fighting. He sent me in his place and says I can keep the money for myself."

By midmorning, Grace realized she had initially underestimated the abilities of her crew. This was simply another day of hard work for these strong and determined farmers.

Although James was the man responsible for organizing the work at hand, Grace proved herself to be a diligent business woman. After memorizing everyone's name in the first fifteen minutes, she carefully observed each man's work ethic.

By 10 o'clock she had the Liberty Table set for tea and cider with some warm cornbread. She invited the oldest third of the workers, whom she assumed would tire first, indoors to take a break. She graciously served them on her finest china, as she easily chatted, addressing each one by name.

"I cannot fit all of you gentlemen at the table at once. Please tell the others after Mrs. Miller and I wash a few cups and make a few more pots of tea, I will invite some more in for their break."

Refreshed and renewed, the men returned cheerfully to work. In this manner, each group took a break without the work coming to a halt. Grace repeated this procedure again for dinner and a mid-afternoon break.

At the end of the first day, the entire yard was not only leveled off, but a two-foot-deep trench was dug completely around the perimeter of the foundation site and the first of the foundation blocks maneuvered into the trench. After some bargaining, a quarter of the workers agreed to return the next day, bringing their own ox team and harness to continue moving granite foundation blocks into the trench. Grace simply paid and sent home any one whom she deemed unable or unwilling to work to her standards. In just three days, James was amazed to find that his entire granite foundation was laid, squared, back-filled and ready to be framed and floored.

Near dawn on the 11th of April, 1781, James awoke earlier than usual and rekindled the day's fire back to life. This was no ordinary day, for it was the beginning of the raising of his family's new home. After years of planning, felling, sectioning, hauling, laying out joints, cutting joinery, splitting shingles, sawing out braces, arranging delivery of granite slabs, measuring, checking and measuring again, it was finally going to be standing upright!

As the new day dawned, he surveyed the timbers, admiring his family's handiwork. He was proud of each one of his sons, for their work ethic, skills and abilities. He was not building this spacious home for himself, but for future generations of Millers.

The evening before, Grace instructed the men in setting up saw horses and planks for "banquet tables". When James protested that he needed the saw horses, Grace informed him that she already instructed the men in town to bring their own.

A few minutes after sunrise, Grace was outside covering her tables with clean linens. She and Sarah were busy setting the tables with all the pewter and china which accompanied Sarah's rustic stoneware dishes.

Two wagons fully loaded with food, tools, sawhorses and planks arrived quickly followed by a succession of neighbors. Half the town believed this new house was a vain extravagance; the other half believed it to be a wise investment. Nearly the entire town turned out that day to work, eat, play music, drink cider and enjoy each other's company.

"Hello neighbor!" and "Good morning, James" was repeated as Fryeburg citizens arrived from near and far in wagons, carts or on foot. James was pleased when Joseph Frye arrived from his farm in the northern end of town. Sarah was smiling brightly as every woman approached her with a dish and every man with a tip of his hat.

"Gentlemen and neighbors," James began, as he saw that most of the town had arrived. He began to call their attentions to the task at hand. "Thank you for coming-offering of your time, muscles and tools to raise our new home. Reverend, would you bless us with a word of prayer before we commence this undertaking."

Following Reverend Fessenden's eloquent invocation, James and Micah divided the men into groups, each to have its own set of responsibilities. The largest group, composed mostly of the stronger men and older boys, would be the lifters. The shorter lifters were stationed at the second floor girt while the taller ones would lift at the third floor girt. There was a lifter stationed wherever there was a space along the frame for them to squeeze in beside each other.

The remaining men of this group would be pike men, hefting wooden poles tipped with a sharp metal spike. They would later join the lifters by jamming their tips into the main girt when these became too high to reach by hand. They were positioned to push the girt up and up until the bent soared over their heads. As each bent reached closer to its own equilibrium, the pike men changed from lifters to holders, keeping it from moving out of balance and falling back down on the deck. There were many more pikes of various lengths than there were pike men; for as the bent slowly rose, lifters would release their holds and quickly pick up a pike and become pike men.

The second group would be in charge of the ropes and blocks to keep the bents from flipping past the upright positions. They were to relieve the lifters of some of the bent's weight as it rose upward, and to prevent the bent posts from sliding off the deck during its ascent. They would also aid the pegging crew by keeping it steady and squarely upright until pegged.

The third group consisted of a mix of experienced men and inexperienced boys. They were responsible for filling lift positions early in the process, then helping wherever needed. They may help plumb a post, organize and test-fit the wall plates and braces, fetch pegs, hammers or mallets, scramble up onto a bent to fit and pound a stubborn joint, or drill and peg.

As the day progressed, James grew attuned to the flow and rhythm of the day; he could see where the parts of the whole were flowing easily or with more difficulty. He had amassed much experience in timber framing barns and homes of friends and neighbors near Boston and along the south shore of Massachusetts. His newer neighbors in the Province of Maine readily acknowledged this experience and often sought his help. Many times his neighbors appointed him as raising master of local projects. Today he did not join a group, but supervised all aspects at once. He took personal responsibility for the safety and efficiency of all the men.

Some of the younger boys, including Benjamin and Ethan, were assigned to help the lifters by pairing up and moving sawhorses in and out as needed. When all the men and boys were finally ready in their positions, James again addressed the groups.

"Hear me, neighbors and friends. Today we are continuing a tradition handed down not just for generations, but for thousands of years in building shelter entirely with our local resources, skills and strength. May our sons continue this tradition with their sons.

Now listen carefully for my instructions. When we are ready to lift, I will repeat these words: READY LIFT, and then LIFT. At that moment, upon the second LIFT, we must put all our backs into it and lift until I call out REST. At this point, let go slowly and the bent will be supported by sawhorses and staging. Horsemen, be ready when you are needed.

When we are ready for the next lift, I will say again READY LIFT and then LIFT. This time I will call upon the pike men to add their stout poles to your muscles. As it rises, longer pikes will be added until it reaches the point of equilibrium.

I will then call for the rope tenders to help slow down its movements and hold it in its upright position as it drops into its mortises with a thump. When we have secured the first bent with spikes into temporary supports, the lifters may enjoy a drink of cider while the wall plates are assembled with their wind braces. When the connections are finished, the next bent will be slid into position against the temporary foot brakes. We will then re-rope, reposition and continue the entire process again."[1]

As the men began their tasks, the women were busy in the kitchen and outdoors. Grace greeted each woman by name. "Mrs. Frye, how lovely of you to come today. Mrs. Dresser, what did you bring that smells so delicious? Mrs. Knight, I am so pleased you are feeling better and able to attend. Thank you so much for coming today, Mrs. Walker. I would dearly love to have your assistance in getting organized."

Every woman, from young girl to great-grandmother, had an important role to play. While watching the younger children, the older girls made sure everyone remained a safe distance from the construction. The elderly made sure the table was properly set and would inform Sarah or Grace if someone needed a refill. Only occasionally did the loud

'Ready Lift-Lift' instruction cause them to stop everything and watch admiringly, yet just a bit fearfully, as another bent was raised to the vertical.

"Grace, dear, you are certainly a gracious hostess," Mrs. Frye complimented.

"Well, it is easy to be a hostess with such delightful guests," she flattered. "However, I must tell you, for me, Mrs. Dresser is the shining example of hospitality," she turned to the modest woman sitting at the far end of the table. "Just imagine hosting twenty Indians overnight! When I was a little girl I had my mother read that letter from Mrs. Miller over and over again. It sounded like such a frightful adventure."

"Not at all, dear. Those Indians were peaceful folk. If you treat them right, they will treat you right," Mrs. Dresser explained.

"Grace, dear, should you be helping Mrs. Miller in the kitchen?" Mrs. Frye reproached.

"Not at all. I must tell you that I have been banished from the hearth since I set my petticoats on fire."

The women roared with laughter. "Your dresses certainly are totally impractical," laughed Mrs. Walker, pointing to Grace's ruffles, ribbons and hoops.

"You do need some sensible clothing," concurred Mrs. Osgood.

"I must tell you that I heartily agree. My own dear mother always said a lady knows how to dress appropriately for the occasion at hand. I do confess that my dresses are totally inappropriate for the rigors of domesticity."

The first two bents were erected and pegged without incident before some of the men took their dinner break. "Mr. Frye, may I pour you some tea?" Grace offered.

"Absolutely not, young lady. I am a Patriot and I shall never drink a drop of tea upon which taxes were paid to that Royal Tyrant, King George!" Joseph Frye loudly proclaimed.

"Neither would I, sir," Grace smiled sweetly. "I assure you that we Peabodys have never paid single pence of tax on this tea. This tea was discreetly imported from Amsterdam."

"The Peabodys are smugglers?" Mr. Walker asked with a new-found respect.

"We prefer the term 'discreet importers'," Grace smiled.

"Then I shall have a second cup," Mr. Evans laughed.

"Young lady, I do like your politics," Mr. Frye admired.

"Oh not at all, Mr. Frye. It is purely a matter of business. The fewer taxes one pays, the larger the profit. The larger the profit, the more ships one can afford to build. More ships result in more imports, which in turn reap higher profits. Building more ships requires hiring more employees, who in turn earn more wages, who can then afford to buy the products we import. It is a simple matter of good business."

"Miss Grace Peabody, please forgive me for interrupting, but we do have a frame to raise," James reminded good naturedly.

"We shall invite all of you back this fall upon the completion of our home," Sarah promised. "We will have plenty of time for talk then."

Hard work and lively discussions made the time pass quickly those two weeks. Not only did the good citizens of Fryeburg raise the Millers' house frame that spring, they also accepted a lonely teenager as one of their own.

IX

A Summer to Remember

A week after planting was done, three wagons filled with carpenters, masons and other workmen with their tools arrived at the Millers' farm one late afternoon. Ethan was the first to run up to the wagons for he was the most excited about this venture. James warmly welcomed the foreman, Mr. John Chamberlain, and his crew.

"Well now, here is the Amazing Grace. You are a pretty little thing just like your mother," the foreman tipped his hat.

"I shall not be patronized, Mr. Chamberlain," she seethed. "I may be pretty like my mother, but I am also smart like my father. I must tell you, sir, it is unbecoming for a man of your station to treat his superiors so disrespectfully. Furthermore, I expect the same level of workmanship that you have provided my father and grandfather. If I receive anything less than your best, none of you shall ever work in Boston again. Have I made myself understood, sir?"

The foreman frowned as he turned crimson, "Yes, Miss Peabody."

With a swish of her petticoats, she headed toward the house. James, always the peacekeeper, said, "Sir, I know you meant no disrespect. I am sure you have children of your own her age; you were just trying to be friendly." Quickly changing the subject, "You can see the frame for yourselves; now let me show you the plans."

Sarah, who silently witnessed Grace's outburst from the dooryard, took Grace by the hand, led her into the house and sat her down at the Liberty Table. She chose her words carefully before speaking.

"Grace, you are not a guest in this home. Mr. Miller and I consider you to be a member of this family. This family maintains Christian standards and morals, one of which is that children are to respect their elders. I would never allow any of my children to display such disrespectful and petty behavior as I just witnessed. I shall certainly not tolerate such outbursts from you.

Mr. Chamberlain is one of the most skilled, master carpenters in Boston and he shall not suffer another outburst from you. You have not only disgraced yourself, you have embarrassed Mr. Chamberlain, Mr. Miller and me as well. You may now retire to your room for the evening; we shall see you in the morning."

"This is a magnificent frame, sir. Did you build this yourself?"

"My three sons and I did this over the course of three winters. Ethan, my youngest here, wants to become a carpenter. He has the desire, the brains and the skills to become a great one, I may add. With your permission he would like to observe and work. Micah is my eldest. I do not know what my back and I would have done without him," he turned and smiled. "He will be spending the summer with me in the fields.

This is Benjamin, my middle son. He is the chief architect and he drew up the plans with input from Miss Peabody. As you can see the house is designed to be in the gable-ended Georgian style with two symmetrical double chimneys. The front of the house will have a central door flanked by a window on each side; the second-floor windows shall be directly above the first-floor windows with a middle window above the door.[1] We have compromised on the style of the moldings around the doors and windows by selecting the Ionic style. It is too fancy for my tastes but not fancy enough for Grace," James laughed good-naturedly. "Benjamin would like to watch your men work—in between doing his chores.

We have made arrangements for you and your men to board with some of the finest families in Fryeburg. I am sure you will all be comfortable. If you wish, you may all leave your tools here in our barn and we shall see all of you first thing in the morning."

Grace had planned for every contingency. She hired several ladies to do the cooking and serving of the dinners and evening meals for the men. Sarah was most grateful. In exchange for James allowing Ethan and Benjamin to spend the summer on the house project, Grace also hired four local teenage boys to work in the fields. Ethan was most grateful.

At the evening meal, no one acknowledged Grace's empty chair or mentioned her outburst. James ate absent-mindedly, for he was lost in his own thoughts.

He had to confess to the Lord his pride. He had always felt inferior to Sarah's family. The Bradfords, direct descendants of Pilgrim William Bradford, were educated, refined and highly respected in the community. On the other hand, his grandfather was a petty criminal in London. He fled England and arrived in Boston as an indentured servant. James' father, Micah Miller, died early, leaving his young widow and their three-year-old son destitute. James's uncle Benjamin, his mother's older brother and successful silversmith, took them in.

"This is America. You have the opportunity to become successful if you work hard enough," his uncle repeated. James never feared hard work, whether it was studying late into the night at Harvard or rising early to plow a field. He took his responsibilities as provider and protector of his family seriously.

Although Sarah was always content with her circumstances, James often felt a tinge of jealousy when his wife read Elizabeth Peabody's letters from Boston. He always thought his Sarah deserved a comfortable home too.

He now realized his decision to build such a large house had not been a wise one. It would have been more prudent to use half the frame to enlarge their humble home to more adequate proportions and the other half to enlarge the barn to a realistic size. He had allowed this situation to grow out of control. Now it was his responsibility to take control of the situation.

Quietly he left the table for Grace's room where she sat on the bed sulking. "I am sorry if my behavior caused you any embarrassment, Mr. Miller," she quietly apologized.

"You need not apologize to me, young lady. However I do expect you will make a public apology to Mr. Chamberlain in the morning."

"Yes, sir."

"You have not only sinned against Mr. Chamberlain, you have sinned against God."

Grace gasped, "Sinned against God?"

"Yes, Grace. God has created all mankind in His image. For you to deem some people inferior to others is a grievous sin."

Grace had never looked at people in that light before.

"In Matthew 6:24 Jesus warns, 'No man can serve two masters; for either he will hate one, and love the other; or he will hold to the one and despise the other. You cannot serve God and mammon'."

"Are you telling me that I cannot do both?" she questioned in confusion. She had never heard this preached from the high, mahogany pulpit in her church in Boston.

James smiled before leaving her room and returning with the family Bible opened to Matthew 19:16. "Perhaps you may wish to spend the evening meditating upon the story of the rich young ruler. You must learn to read the Scriptures for yourself and not simply listen to other people expound their own ideas."

Grace had never touched a Bible; now she was to spend an evening reading from and meditating upon one.

"Grace, I am thankful for your generosity in building this house. However a house is not a home unless there is love and respect in the family. In the future, if you have a concern with one of the workers please discreetly bring the matter to my attention. It is my responsibility to handle such matters.

I am also grateful for your companionship to Mrs. Miller. I know you have brought much comfort and joy to her life. Please remember, Grace, that Mrs. Miller is the mistress of this home, not you. Tomorrow is a new day. I bid you good night."

The entire crew arrived the next morning at sunrise. Grace briskly approached Mr. Chamberlain, "Mr. Chamberlain, sir, I do ask your forgiveness for my un-lady like behavior yesterday. I must tell you that only my father calls me by his pet name of 'The Amazing Grace'. I do not wish for others to display such familial behavior."

"Miss Peabody, I shall gladly accept your apology if you will accept my sincerest condolences for your loss. I have the highest respect for your family. Please excuse me now, Miss Peabody, for we have a house to build," he smiled before turning away.

Immediately, the masons and their assistants began their preparations for building the two large, double-sided fireplaces and chimneys. The chief mason was already searching out areas of the best local clay to be found in or around Fryeburg. The house that James was building used only 6 of the original 8 bents of the intended barn, so there were extra timbers, some a good 40-feet long, stacked to the side of the building site. These timbers, split or sawed into smaller sections, would be turned into useful lumber for the house or saved for a barn addition. Some of the carpenters began to turn much of the remaining framing members into temporary staging, as well as an elevated trestle for the pit saw to turn logs and extra timbers into boards. Other necessary contraptions to be created were foot-powered wood lathes, sawhorses, shaving horses, and various workbenches that were not practical to ship north along with the men and their tools.

Within a week of their arrival, carpenters were marking out, notching for, and securing the evenly spaced studs, sheathing the roof and framing the doors and windows. Several weeks later—when the two chimneys were protruding through the top of the frame—the carpenters had studded all two and a half floors, had installed a good portion of the subflooring and began nailing the white pine clapboards which James had so carefully crafted. Wherever one turned in the Millers' yard that summer, there was a carpenter, mason, laborer, teamster, cook, farmer, or neighbor doing his or her part to complete the house by the end of August.

Ethan learned how to use a clapboard gauge to insure that the overlap of each row remained constant.[2] However, he discovered that nailing clapboards and shingling the roof was exhausting and tedious work.

It was not all work that summer; Grace turned mundane, daily meals into social events. In addition to the Miller family, there were the five Fryeburg ladies cooking and serving the meals, the four field hands and the building crew from Boston. Laughter, tall tales, and gossip were served with the beans and cornbread. Curious town folk would often drop by to observe the progress. The locals were enthralled

with the stories of city life. In turn, the Bostonians admired
the resourcefulness and creativity of Fryeburg's citizens. Mr.
Chamberlain often admitted that the presence of both Grace
and Sarah helped to keep swearing and rude language to a
record low level.

Ethan befriended a young man from Ireland, a skilled car-
penter named Daniel Merrill, who boarded with the Millers.
He took the time to supervise and critique Ethan's skills.
Daniel was shingling near the peak of the roof one glorious
and sunny day, when Grace shouted from the ground, "Mr.
Merrill, are you enjoying the view from up there?"

"Yes, Miss. I mean no, Miss."

"I would thank you to work for your wages, good sir.
You may spend the Sabbath afternoon on the roof enjoying
the majestic scenery. Please give your labors your undivided
attention." With a swish of her petticoats, she was gone;
Ethan and Daniel burst into laughter.

As half the crew was shingling the roof, the other half
was nailing 14 inch wide pumpkin pine boards for the
flooring over the rough subfloors. Because these craftsmen
were accustomed to shipbuilding, the flooring was joined
together by ship-lap joints.[3]

Ethan discovered he enjoyed the indoor, detailed
finish carpentry. The walls of both the drawing room and
dining room were to be wainscoted with wooden panels.
Mr. Chamberlain was duly impressed with Ethan's skill in
planing and framing each oak panel. Building interior doors
became his forte; each door with two long rectangular panels
on the top and two shorter rectangular panels on the bottom
was constructed like a piece of fine furniture.[4]

While Ethan was busy making doors with some of the
more skilled carpenters, the rest of the crew were finishing
the interior walls. The house wrights nailed oak lathing to the
studs before plastering. Initially Grace insisted that the ceil-
ings be plastered as well. James rejected that notion imme-

diately, stating the extra time and expense was prohibitive if they intended to complete the project on time and on budget. However the brothers understood that Father was justifiably proud of this timber frame and did not wish to envelope his masterpiece in a layer of plaster.

In early August, James received word that *The Amazing Grace* had docked in Falmouth with a shipment of windows and hardware. Grace hired Mr. Swan, Mr. Bradley and Mr. Knight with their teams of oxen and wagons to pick them up and deliver them to the farm.

Framing and installing all the windows transformed the house from a construction site to a home. Ethan was fascinated by the unfamiliar hardware. He grew up seeing butterfly hinges on cupboard doors and trunks and the stronger H-hinges on doors, but he had never seen the H-L hinge before. Daniel explained that this hinge was capable of carrying larger and heavier doors than the H-hinge while the L extension kept the door frame square.[5]

Ethan was already familiar with Suffolk latches and simple arrowhead handles found in all of the homes in Fryeburg and most of the homes in New England. Daniel explained that these unfamiliar and ornate handles were called swordfish handles because the tops and bottoms came to a long sharp point like a swordfish[6] Ethan appreciated the blacksmith's skill in making such intricate designs and surmised that this style of handle must be popular with the seafaring folk.

Ethan was allowed to help build the narrow, back staircase which led from the new "work room" to the back of the second floor. Only Mr. Chamberlain, Daniel and two other master carpenters built the master staircase which would greet visitors as they entered the foyer through the front door. Unlike the back staircase, these stairs had a longer, more gradual angle of ascent with wider treads and lower risers.

The newel post was handsomely carved with ornate designs. A gleaming handrail rested upon gracefully turned balusters.[7]

It was the last week of August and as the workmen were running out of time, Grace was running out of money. *The Amazing Grace* was due to arrive in Falmouth loaded with all of Grace's worldly possessions and the workers were expected to be there to meet the ship if they wanted a ride back to Boston. The plaster was quickly whitewashed with quick lime and water.[8] The wainscoting in the dining room was painted moss green; the wainscoting in the drawing room was painted yellow ochre. Grace lamented they were unable to wallpaper[9] Sarah consoled her by suggesting they could stencil the rooms in the future.

The vast upstairs would remain unfinished, with no interior walls, no plaster and no finished flooring. After sleeping in the crowded loft, the brothers assured Grace that sleeping upstairs, albeit an unfinished one would be a treat.

Half the town attended a farewell supper the evening before the Bostonians' departure. Grace publicly thanked Mr. Chamberlain and his crew for a job well done. "Upon the completion of building a ship, we christen it and give it a new name. Mr. Miller, with your approval I would like to christen this house with the name 'Riverview Farm'." The town's people applauded with approval.

James warmly invited them to come back and visit the family any time for they had plenty of room. Ethan protested when Daniel gave him a set of woodcarving chisels. "A carpenter is only as good as his tools. Besides, I intend to buy myself a new set in Boston with some of my wages."

Ten men volunteered to drive their ox teams and wagons to deliver the workmen with their tools to Falmouth and to return with Grace's furniture. Grace was thankful for their altruism for she had spent the last of her shillings. The truth was they were curious to see *The Amazing Grace* and get a close look at her belongings.

James allowed the brothers to accompany him on this adventure; Sarah forbade Grace to go stating it would be improper for her to travel alone in the company of so many men. In deference to Grace's hurt feelings, Micah offered to stay home and care for the livestock. Her grateful smile was reward enough for his sacrifice.

Sarah, Micah, Grace and several neighbors eagerly greeted the returning wagon train that September. Each piece of furniture was expertly wrapped in canvas and packed in straw-filled wooden crates. Each crate was carefully opened and Grace instructed the men to the location of each piece of furniture.

"We shall begin with the dining room, gentlemen. First the table." Ethan had never imagined that such furniture existed. It took six men to carry the Georgian, ten-foot, pedestal mahogany table which comfortably seated twelve and place it in the center of the room. The brothers carried in twelve fan-backed chairs with moss green, velvet upholstered seats. A six-foot wide, mahogany sideboard was placed between the two windows. The lower half had three rows of drawers; the upper half had three large shelves. Ethan thought it looked like a bookcase for dishes. The matching side table with four drawers was placed against the opposite wall.[9]

When Grace was satisfied with the arrangement, she turned her attention to the drawing room. It took three men to carry the Chippendale tall clock and two men to carry the matching writing desk from the original part of the house to their proper places; the desk was in front of the fire place and the clock in an interior corner. How Ethan admired the desk's four, gracefully curved legs with intricate carvings.

Benjamin eagerly helped carry in the two matching book cases which flanked each side of the fireplace. He imagined the books which would fill the lower shelves hidden behind wooden doors and the upper shelves displayed behind glass doors.

There was much discussion as to where to place the two winged back chairs and the intricately carved mahogany, Tudor styled settel. Finally, it was Sarah who took command of the situations and decided that the chairs upholstered in colorful, intricate needle point were placed by the windows of the side wall. The settel upholstered in white fabric with gold designs was placed along the front wall between the windows. Micah thought the designs looked like wheat sheaves.[10]

Grace was thrilled when her bedroom furniture was uncrated. Her four-poster bed with a frame for a canopy was moved in first, then two matching bedside cabinets. Her grandmother's 1710 William and Mary highboy was placed by the fireplace; her mother's dressing table with the looking glass added the final touch[11]

William and Elizabeth's four poster bed was moved into the front bedroom for James and Sarah. James emphatically declined the canopy and bed curtains. The Chippendale armoire which Grace brought with her in March was placed against the outside wall; Sarah selected a chest of drawers with four rows of drawers carved with grapevines and leaves. Elizabeth's writing desk of dark chocolate brown mahogany finished with gold gilding was placed at an angle in the corner.[12]

Ethan never realized that hallways had furniture. An Elizabethan oak chest was placed in the foyer just before the door to the drawing room. Sarah announced it was perfect to store mittens, muffs, hats. Above the chest, Micah hung a looking glass with a mahogany fluted frame. Across the hall at the foot of the stairs was an oak wardrobe with double doors. The family's cloaks and great coats were removed from their pegs and into the wardrobe.[13]

All the remaining furniture was carried up the grand staircase to the vacant second floor. Three four-poster beds, six chests of drawers, five wardrobes, six unopened trunks filled with treasures, and two bookcases were delivered in a haphazard manner by the exhausted men.

The last three crates held woven carpets imported from Holland[14] No amount of cajoling or pleading by Grace could convince the volunteers to remove the downstairs furniture, lay the carpets and replace the furniture. Sarah suggested they carry the carpets upstairs and deal with it another day.

Sixty years later the old timers still reminisced about that summer. It was a turning point in Ethan's life for it was the summer in which he decided to become a furniture maker. He intended to become America's version of Thomas Chippendale.

X

The Beauty of Autumn

N othing went to waste at Riverview Farm; Micah used the discarded straw for clean bedding for the live-stock; Benjamin saved the broken crates for kindling; Grace nailed the canvas to the studs on the second floor to make "walls". It took three evenings, two creative women and four Millers to arrange rugs and to arrange furniture, to rearrange rugs and to rearrange furniture on the second floor to form three 'bedrooms'.

Micah selected the back portion—closest to the back staircase—so he could easily slip out the back door and go to the barn without disturbing anyone. Grace helped him select one bed, a chest of drawers, a trunk which he used as a table and a wardrobe. He was pleased when Grace spent half an evening selecting just the right sheets, pillow shams, blan-kets and quilt for his bed.

Benjamin chose the front section closest to the grand staircase. He and James placed the two book cases to serve as a divider. Benjamin placed his books in a few shelves and dreamed of the day he would have enough books to fill both book cases. He and Sarah selected one wardrobe, two chests of drawers and a trunk at the foot of his four poster bed. Grace and Sarah were both delighted when he agreed to the royal blue, damask canopy and bed curtains which matched the royal blue and white comforter. He thought it looked like a bed a famous attorney would sleep in.

Ethan, who was secretly afraid of the dark, was grateful to set up his furniture in the center, with his older brothers guarding each staircase. He allowed Sarah and Grace to place any of the remaining furniture the way they wished. He was more concerned about displaying his extensive rock collection on the tops of two trunks, his bird nest collection on the top of his wardrobe and a variety of baskets throughout the upstairs. The second floor may have been unfinished but the brothers thought they slept in a mansion.

One bright, late September morning while Sarah and Grace were preparing breakfast Sarah stated, "Today is a perfect day to dye."

"Mrs. Miller, what a terrible thing to say! Your family loves you! We need you!"

Sarah laughed so hard she almost dropped a kettle. "Thank you, it is good to know that I am loved and needed. I did not say it is a good day to be dead. I said it is a good day to dye some fleece."

"Can we dye some fleece pink? I would love to have a pink shawl."

"I am sorry to disappoint you, Grace, but there are no plants that I know of that produce red or pink dye."

"Well, the British soldiers back in Boston all wore red uniforms. Where did the red dye come from?"

"From crushed cochineal insects."

"From dead bugs? I must tell you that is disgusting!"

"I was thinking of tan and brown for work clothes. You could use a few sensible work dresses and James needs a new great coat. We could also dye some fleece yellow; that would make a lovely shawl. You may pick some goldenrod in the fields while I mordant the fleece. Put the leafy shoots in one basket and the yellow flowers in another. A little fresh air will do us both some good."

Micah helped his mother set out her large iron dye pot outdoors, drew buckets of water from the well and poured four gallons of water for every pound to fleece into the pot. While her clean, carded fleece soaked in a large tin tub for an hour, Sarah measured tablespoons of alum and teaspoons of cream of tartar and dissolved them in a pan of hot water. James lit a small fire under the pot before he and his sons set out to harvest some beans, squash, carrots and beets. Sarah hummed to herself as she added the mordant to the pot and stirred. An hour later she added the wet fleece and let the pot simmer for another hour.[1]

Meanwhile, Grace was enjoying her freedom and solitude as she picked goldenrod in the fields. Back in Boston she was not allowed to step outdoors without her mother or a proper chaperone. She was beginning to appreciate the simplicity of life in Fryeburg and to respect the resourcefulness of the townspeople. She returned home with rosy cheeks and two large baskets brimming with goldenrod. As the fleece was cooling in the backyard, the family enjoyed their dinner.

"Shall we dye with yellow first?" Grace asked eagerly.

"While I clean up the kitchen, put the yellow flowers in the dye pot, cover them with water and let it simmer for half an hour. Be mindful of the flames!" Sarah warned.

A half an hour later, they strained the flowers out of the water, added some mordanted fleece and ten minutes later they were rewarded with golden yellow fleece.[2] "I must tell you, Mrs. Miller, this is lovely. Shall we do another batch while we still have the dye?"

As two batches of yellow fleece dried in the sunshine, they repeated the process with the leafy shoots to make brown.[3] By sunset their newly dyed fleece was neatly packed in a trunk ready for their winter projects. A contented Grace slept well that night ready to pick more goldenrod the next day.

After Ethan and Grace spent a warm September morning picking apples, she convinced Sarah to spend the afternoon peeling and coring apples out doors in the sunshine. Micah threw the discarded apple peels into the compost pile as they strung rows of apple slices on linen thread and hung them over the mantel to dry.

The next morning the ladies picked baskets of mint, chamomile, lemon balm, sage, thyme and comfrey and spent another pleasant afternoon tying them in bunches to hang upside down from a kitchen beam. When completely dried, they would be stored in stoneware crocks, labeled and placed in Abigail's old bedroom which currently served as their new pantry.

Preparing for winter was serious business. The men worked from sunrise to sunset filling the root cellar and chopping and stacking more firewood in the woodshed. Micah bartered one half cord of firewood for two fur pelts which he intended to make mittens. In the evening Benjamin would read aloud from *Gulliver's Travels* while Sarah spun flax to make linen and Grace knitted stockings. Everyone knew the fleeting beauty of autumn would soon be replaced with the cold reality of winter.

Grace thought there was nothing more beautiful than an October afternoon. Mornings and evenings were getting colder, but sunny afternoons were perfect to take a stroll down the lane and observe all of creation prepare for winter.

Ethan taught her to recognize the trees by their leaves and she sketched them into her journal. By far, the maple leaves were the most colorful. She wished she had learned to paint like John Singleton Copley, for she would have painted the many colors found in the brilliant foliage on the snowcapped mountains. Squirrels were scurrying, collecting acorns for the winter while the Canadian Geese flew overhead, all flying south in perfect V-shaped forms. She knew she would need to return home soon for everyone was needed at harvest time, but today she would enjoy a few peaceful moments by the river.

"Sarah, it looks like we both received letters today," James handed her a letter from Abigail. With a mug of cider in one hand and the letter in the other, Sarah sat down at the dining room table to read.

> *Braintree, Massachusetts*
> *September, 1781*
>
> *My Dearest Sarah,*
>
> *It was with much joy I read your last letter. I am so grateful that our little Grace has found a loving home. To think she is learning to cook, care for the sheep and chickens, make maple sugar, churn butter, plant a garden, card fleece and now learn to spin! Only you, my friend, would have the loving patience to teach her these skills.*
>
> *The new house must be beautiful and I long for the day that my family and I will come to visit. I would have loved to watch her supervising the workmen. I think Grace will grow up to be an indomitable business woman in her own right.*
>
> *John, John Quincy and Charles are no longer in Holland. John has returned to Paris and Charles will be returning home! John has not informed me as to when and how.[4] I do wish he returns before the winter's stormy seas set in. But it will be so good to have him home!*
>
> *But alas John Quincy has accompanied Francis Dana to St. Petersburg, Russia to serve as his interpreter and secretary.[5] I understand that his French is superb. I know I should be proud, but Russia is half a world away!*

I do envy you, Sarah, for having your family with you and watching your sons grow up before your very eyes. Do write soon. Your letters lift my spirits.
Affectionately,
Abigail

James took his letter into the drawing room and sat down at the Chippendale desk.

Boston, Massachusetts
October, 1781

Dear Mr. Miller,
I regret to inform you that Mr. William Francis Peabody II died peacefully in his sleep last night after suffering a debilitating stroke the week before. I am writing to ascertain that the household furnishings did arrive safely at Falmouth and now in your possession.

I beg your pardon for overstepping my boundaries, but William was a dear personal friend as well as a business rival and I wish to inquire about the well-being of Grace, his only grandchild.

According to William's will, the business and all of his wealth is to be evenly divided between his son William and his nephew Thomas. In William's absence, Thomas is taking over all business and financial matters and intends to sell Mr. Peabody's mansion and auction off the contents of the house. He claims the business needs the money in order to stay solvent during these difficult war years.

Unfortunately, he does not feel obligated to share any of the proceeds with Grace, He states if her father returns, he shall care for her himself or if William is legally declared dead in a few years, Grace shall be entitled to whatever is stipulated in his will.

At the age of ninety-three, William was aware that he did not have much longer to live. That is why after Elizabeth's death, he insisted that Grace go live with you. It would have been an easier transition if Grace had simply moved in with Abigail Adams. However, William was concerned for his granddaughter's safety. In the event that the British win this war, John Adams will be tried and hanged for treason. He felt his granddaughter would be safer living with a less notorious family far away from Boston and removed from politics. He did his best to provide for her.
            Sincerely,
            John Hancock

James and Sarah quietly discussed the contents of their letters and the best way to approach Grace with the news. Grace had lost a great deal and Sarah feared how she would respond to the loss of her grandfather and the distance of her closest friend.

The evening meal was served in the dining room.

"It is not Sunday," Ethan observed. "Are we having company?"

"Just the family," Sarah smiled at Grace. Everyone stood at their seats while James prayed. "Almighty God, grant us grateful hearts for all Thy blessings and provisions. We thank Thee for this family and for keeping us safely together. There are so many families on both sides of the Atlantic that are torn apart. We thank Thee for a bountiful harvest. There are so many families who are going hungry. We thank Thee for this home and for Grace who made it possible. There are many tonight who are in need of warmth and shelter. May this home be filled with love and gratitude and be a refuge for those in need. Amen."

Micah and Benjamin sensed something was wrong. Ethan joyfully filled his plate with food.

"I do believe that I am getting back my appetite," Sarah smiled. "I know this past year has been extremely trying for each of us. But I am so grateful to have all of you. I received the most distressing letter today from my dear friend Abigail. John has left Holland for Paris and she has no idea when she will ever see him again. They have been apart more than they have been together since their marriage. I am so grateful to have your father home. I simply do not know how I would have managed this year without him. I do not know how Abigail does it.

I am so grateful to have my sons living at home with me and to be able to watch them grow. Poor Abigail misses Charles and John Quincy so much. She does not even know where Charles is. This summer he left for home and no one has heard from him or knows his whereabouts. And if that is not enough, John Quincy and Francis Dana are on their way to Russia."

Benjamin put his spoon down. He spent the day hauling water from the well, stacking firewood and feeding livestock. John Quincy is traveling across Europe heading toward the palace of Catherine the Great. How can life be so unfair!

In her most dignified tone of voice Grace commented, "I am most looking forward to John Quincy's next letter. I am sure he will have much to tell. Perhaps I should correspond with Mrs. Adams as well. I believe she will be much amused to learn I am becoming quite domestic."

At the end of the meal James turned to his sons, "Gentlemen, please clean up for your mother this evening. She and I and Grace will take our tea in the drawing room."

"Grace, dear I received a letter from Mr. Hancock today," James began.

"Oh, so this is what all of this is about. You are going to tell me that my grandfather died. He was ninety-three years of age and in failing health. Why else would Mr. Hancock write?"

"Yes, dear, I am afraid so."

"Must I be present when they read the will?"

"No, that will not be necessary" Sarah cleared her throat. "Your grandfather cared about you very much. He sent his carpenters to build the house; he sent your family's possessions to fill it. He wanted to be assured that you were well provided for. Do you know why he sent you to us?"

"Yes, my mother no longer associated with her family. Living with the Aldens was not an option. Mrs. Adams is too busy to take on the responsibility of raising another child."

"Dear Grace, he was concerned for your safety. He knew he had not much time left and would not be here to protect you. He felt your life might be endangered if the British won the war and you were living with such a high profile Patriot family like the Adams. Every decision he made was with your best interests in mind."

"And my inheritance?" she asked impatiently.

"If your father returns after the war, he shall continue to financially provide for you. If your father does not return in a few more years, he shall be declared legally dead. At that time his will shall be read."

"Are you telling me I have nothing? Nothing!" she screamed.

"Grace, dear," Sarah spoke softly. "You have suffered much loss this past year. However, you are not left with nothing. You have a beautiful home to live in, your home. You have beautiful furniture and treasures - all memories of your parents. Above all you have us. We love you, Grace."

James felt compassion. "Lay not up for yourselves treasures upon earth, where moth and rust doth corrupt, and where thieves break through and steal. For where your treasure is, there will your heart be also."

145

Grabbing a candle, Grace fled the house in tears and ran into the barn where her black wooly friend greeted her. She climbed over the gate, jumped into the hay and sobbed. She did not hear Micah silently enter.

"Grace, I am so sorry about your grandfather. Please do not worry. Everything we have belongs to you too. This is your home too. You can live with us for as long as you like."

"Go away, Micah! Leave me alone!"

"You are more valuable than the sum of your possessions, Grace. You do not need silk and satin dresses to be beautiful. You are beautiful, Grace."

"Go away," she sniffed.

"I cannot," he sprinted over the gate and sat in the hay beside her. "Here is your cloak. Mother says you will catch your death of a cold. Father told me to take the candle before you burn the barn down."

One unintended consequence of having a large home was the family no longer spent their evenings together. Ethan spent most of his evenings weaving baskets or whittling in the work room. Sarah, who preferred the warmth of the hearth, moved her spinning wheel out of the work room back into the kitchen. Grace would card fleece by Sarah's side for several hours before retiring into the privacy of her bedroom. Feeling like a wealthy gentlemen farmer, James enjoyed the luxury of sitting at the dining room table by a fire sipping cider and keeping records of his crops and his accounts. Micah, who by far worked physically harder than his brothers, went to his bed, lying under a pile of blankets and quilts appreciating the temporary solitude of having the entire upstairs to himself. Benjamin would sit at the Chippendale desk in the drawing room, reading while pretending he was a famous attorney working in his distinguished office.

One November evening the tall clock struck eight when Grace brought in a cup of tea to Benjamin reading *Arabian Nights* in his "office".

"For me? Why thank you, Grace."

"Are you enjoying my father's book?"

"Absolutely."

"You spend a great deal of your evenings in this room," she observed.

"Well, it is an elegant and peaceful room conducive to study. It is my sanctuary from farm life," he confided.

"You hypocrite!" she snarled. "This room and everything in it was furnished by and I quote 'a smuggler and a slave trader'. I do not hear you protesting now, do I?"

Benjamin stood up and looked her in the eyes, "You think you are better than everybody because you are rich!"

"Well, you think you are better than everybody because you are so smart!"

"Well, you are not rich anymore! And I am still smart!"

James and Sarah entered the drawing room just in time to see Grace slap Benjamin across the face. If not for the presence of his parents, he would have slapped her back.

"Grace Alden Peabody! Go to your room," Sarah scolded.

"I certainly will not!" she defied. "This is MY house and I shall do as I please!"

"Young lady," James began.

"I shall handle this, dear. A lady controls her anger. Her anger shall not control her. Is this how a Peabody behaves - like some drunken bar maid who insults and slaps people as she pleases?"

Grace stood speechless, angry, humiliated and contrite.

Suddenly there was the sound of hoof beats and a fevered pounding on the front door.

"Mercy!" Sarah exclaimed, fearful of the worse. Ethan and Micah ran into the foyer in time to see James open the door to let in an impatient, disheveled Moses Ames.

"Did you hear? Did you hear?" Mr. Ames panted. "Cornwallis surrendered to George Washington a few days ago at York Town, Virginia.[5]

The war is over! We won!"

"Moses, please do come in," James invited.

"That is all I know. The war is over. I am on my way to Dr. Emery's to spread the word" He hopped back on his horse and rode off in the moonlight.

XI

A Very Long Winter

By January 1, James declared they would run out of firewood within six to eight weeks. "This house is simply too large to heat."

"How can we run out of firewood? Look at all the trees," Grace nodded out the dining room window.

"It is not like the trees chop themselves down and throw themselves into the fireplace," Benjamin, who hated chopping firewood, gasped in exasperation.

"James, of course you are right." interjected Sarah. "For the winter we shall close off the drawing room, the dining room and the work room. We have plenty of blankets and quilts we can add to our beds."

Once again, the Millers spent their winter evenings around the Liberty Table by the hearth with Grace carding fleece, Sarah spinning and Ethan weaving baskets. However, no one sat quietly reading, for everyone discussed the end of the war.

"Father, will we now have an American king?" Ethan asked one evening.

"No, we shall never have a king."

"Who will rule us, then? Every country has a king or an emperor."

"We are free men and we shall rule ourselves," Micah proudly stated.

"But that has never been done before."

"Our forefather William Bradford signed the Mayflower Compact while crossing the Atlantic," Benjamin explained. "He wrote all about it later in his history book entitled *Of Plymouth Plantation*. They drew up a social contract which free men voluntarily agreed to follow. They planned their future government with just and equal laws. This contract was based on the original Biblical covenant between God and the Israelites.[1]

Grace had to admit that even she was impressed with Benjamin's knowledge of the subject.

"We already have thirteen colonies—I mean states—with governors and state constitutions. That should be enough," Micah stated.

"Not so, Micah," Benjamin disagreed. "That would make us thirteen little countries. We cannot be the separate states of America. We need to be the United States of America."

"I must tell you Benjamin, I agree." added Grace. "We must legally become one sovereign nation and be recognized as such by other nations before we can set up trade agreements. And what about currency? Do we still use the British pound sterling? We certainly cannot continue to use the worthless continental dollar. Also, each state cannot print its own currency for trade would be too confusing between the states, let alone other trading countries. We must have one currency for the entire nation in order to conduct interstate commerce."

"Spoken like a true Peabody," Benjamin complimented.

James continued, "We have thirteen colonies now—I mean states. But what about all of the land west of the Appalachian Mountains? Who controls that? Will they become one giant 14th state?"

"Will we have navigational rights to the Mississippi River? Papa says as the population grows and moves west, we will need the Mississippi for travel and commerce. We cannot do that if the British still own it."

"What about the war debts? Who will be responsible for those?" Benjamin asked. "Are the individual states? Will each state establish its own army? We need some kind of general government over the state government. We must elect a leader who supersedes the governors. If he fails to do the will of the people, we need not go to war, we shall elect another leader."

"According to Abigail's latest letter, those are the issues that John, Benjamin Franklin and John Jay are working on in Paris," Sarah explained.[2]

"Well, I wish they would hurry up. I want Papa to come home."

"So do I Grace. So do I." Benjamin solemnly concurred.

The first week of January brought a blizzard and bitter cold. Only James and Micah braved the elements to care for the livestock in the barn. Yet no one remained idle.

Micah was making three pairs of bear- fur mittens while Ethan wove a small egg basket for Grace. Benjamin was silently reviewing his Greek verbs as James repaired some leather harnesses. Grace was combing flax on a hackle[3] as Sarah spun the flax into linen on her small spinning wheel.

Grace interrupted the silence. "What was Abigail like?"

"She looked just like Benjamin, only she was a girl," Ethan explained.

"Since Benjamin with his dark brown hair and eyes, looks like his mother, then Abigail must have looked like you, Mrs. Miller."

"Well, she did favor the Bradford side of the family," Sarah agreed. "She was always joyful, singing or humming when she did her chores."

"Abigail never complained," Benjamin glared at Grace. "She was often sick and could not go outdoors to play, but she never complained. She was patient and always thankful when I sat down and read to her."

"She never thought of herself more highly than others," Micah continued. "It was Abigail who taught Limbo about the Bible and suggested that Benjamin teach him how to read."

"She was kind, compassionate and thoughtful, just like her mother," James warmly smiled at his wife.

"She would have loved you," Sarah laughed. "She would have loved dressing in your clothes and teaching you to do her chores. I am very grateful that you have grown fond of her sheep. She would have appreciated that." After a moment of uncomfortable silence, she added "I take comfort that I spent every day of Abigail's life with her and was with her when she died. Your grandmother must be heartbroken over the death of her daughter, your mother."

"You know my Grandmother Alden?"

"Do I know her? Goodness, I spent half of my child-hood at her house. She gave the best parties—not like John Hancock of course. She had a way of turning the mundane events into celebrations. If a new foal was born, she would have tea and biscuits in the dining room. When we children recovered from the mumps, she invited my family plus the Smiths to her home for a fancy dinner. She claimed the house had been too quiet while we were all home sick in our beds and she needed a little laughter and mischief. When it came to mischief, your mother was always the center of it all."

"My mother?" Grace laughed. "My prim and proper mother was into mischief? Please, do tell."

"One hot and humid summer day—we must have been nine or ten years old—your mother was furious because your grandmother forbade us to go swimming with our brothers in a nearby pond. As soon as your grandmother turned her back, Elizabeth ran down to the pond."

"Did you go too, mother?" Benjamin interrupted.

She blushed, "Of course I did. Well, we stole all the boys' clothing which they had left on shore and we hid behind a tree. Our brothers had no choice but to run all the way home buck naked!"

"Mercy!" Grace gasped. James and Micah roared with laughter while Benjamin blushed crimson.

"You are not alone, Grace Alden Peabody. You have two grandparents, aunts and uncles and cousins you have never met. My mother informed them that you are now living with us. I am sure your grandmother would cherish receiving a letter from you."

"I shall write a letter to them this evening," Grace promised. This was the beginning of a life-long correspondence.

The next morning at breakfast James announced, "Today we shall slaughter another pig. We have the entire winter to safely freeze the pork."

Micah saw the expression of dismay in Grace's eyes. "Do not be alarmed. Father and I will slaughter and butcher the pig out in the barn."

"I will be happy to help Mother and Grace make the sausage," Ethan volunteered.

"I shall return to my studies," Benjamin looked hopefully to his father. To his relief, James smiled and nodded.

After dinner Micah brought in a large platter of one inch strips of raw pork and fat. Grace felt her stomach turn, as he placed the platter down on the Liberty Table. Dutifully she placed small bowls containing herbs and spices on the table, trying not to look at the meat. Sarah placed a large bowl filled with water and long, white, slimy objects.

"What is that? "

"These are pig intestines. We shall use them for the casing of the sausage," Sarah casually explained.

"I think not."

"Grace, where do you think sausage comes from?"

"In Boston they came from the butcher's shop. I must tell you that I am not touching that," she pointed to the bowl, "or that" she pointed to the platter.

"Today, you may watch Ethan and me. This is definitely a two person job and I may need you in the future. However, you may make yourself useful by adding the herbs and spices to the meat."

She took 6 teaspoons of pepper followed by 6 teaspoons of salt and evenly sprinkled them over the meat. She continued with 2 teaspoons of mace and 2 teaspoons of cloves. She grated one nutmeg and sprinkled the powder, and added 2 tablespoons of sage and 1 teaspoon of marjoram. Sarah poured 1 cup of water evenly over the platter.

Ethan attached a four inch long cylinder, one inch in diameter to the meat grinder. Skillfully Sarah slid the intestine over the cylinder, before placing one slice after the other in the top of the grinder. Ethan continuously turned the handle and the ground pork filled the intestine or casing. Every four inches, Sarah would twist the casing tightly and continue the process. This continued for hours until every last scrap of meat was used.[4]

That evening the Millers enjoyed a fine meal of fried link sausage and potatoes. Grace excused herself and retired early.

The Saco River had frozen over and the weather had moderated. James and his sons were planning to chop down hardwood trees for next winter's firewood. As Micah left for the barn to harness the oxen to the sled, Sarah asked, "Benjamin, do you feel strong enough for such rigorous work?"

He had to choose between spending the day in relative comfort and warmth and listening to Grace's chatter or enduring the cold with his brothers. "I have my new fur mittens. I shall be fine."

"Sarah, his illness was a year ago. A boy his age needs fresh air and exercise," James reassured her as they left.

"Today, we shall make candles, Grace. Please begin tying five wicks, equally spaced, to each of these willow sticks," Sarah instructed.

"There must be at least fifty sticks here. We are going to make two hundred and fifty candles today?"

"Yes, and we shall make an additional two hundred and fifty candles tomorrow, as well. In the past we needed one candle per day. Now, with all the additional rooms, we shall need more." Sarah placed some rags on the floor before setting two high back chairs facing opposite directions approximately three feet apart. "After tying the wicks on a stick, please lay each stick across the backs of these chairs. I shall melt the tallow."

"Tallow? What is tallow?"

"Tallow is beef or mutton fat."

"I must tell you that is disgusting."

"It is not disgusting. We are being responsible stewards of the resources which God has provided. Did you not know where candles come from?"

"In Boston they came from the Chandler's Shop."

Sarah laughed as she stirred the tallow in the cast iron pot over the flames. "Please help me render the tallow. We shall pour the melted fat through this cloth to strain the impurities such as bits of bones and fur." Grace made a face, as she assisted in the distasteful task.

"Now, we shall take one of your sticks with five wicks and quickly dip them into this pot of tallow, return the stick across the backs of the chairs and take the next stick. When we get to the last stick, we shall continue the process all day until each candle is sufficiently thick enough.[5]

"This is boring," Grace complained.

"Oh no, Grace, only boring people get bored," Sarah chastised. "Do you wish to hear of more adventures of Sarah Bradford and Elizabeth Alden?"

"Please, do tell!"

Two days later, the Millers had a good year's supply of candles stored in the tin candle safe and Grace discovered she loved the mischievous young Elizabeth Alden. All that winter she wrote letters to her aunts requesting more tales of her mother's youthful adventures.

After breakfast one day, the Miller men left for another day in the woods. "Today, Grace, we shall make the men new shifts," Sarah instructed, as she rolled yards of new linen cloth across the Liberty Table.

"But I do not know how to sew," Grace protested.

"Last week, you did not know how to make candles either, but you learned. Your mother and I were cutting out and sewing shifts when we were ten years old."

"My mother sewed?"

"Indeed she did, and so shall you. The shift is basically one piece of fabric with a hole cut out in the center for the head to go through," she explained as she drew an outline of the garment in chalk. "Now, I shall draw out two sets of longer and wider ones for James and Micah than I do for the younger boys. Please cut this out as I continue to lay out the garments.

"I certainly prefer this to dipping candles," Grace admitted as she carefully cut out the fabric.

"Both chores are equally necessary. You are doing a fine job. Please continue cutting as I set the beans to soak, churn the butter and make the cornbread."

Grace completed her task just as Sarah was placing the pan of cornbread batter into the coals to bake. "Now I shall sketch the sleeves and underarm gussets. When these are done we shall spend the rest of the day sewing."[6]

"May we start a fire in the drawing room, pour a cup of tea, and sew sitting in the upholstered, wing backed chairs?" Grace asked hopefully.

"I do believe that it would be most pleasant to sit in the sunshine and enjoy the view of the river as we sew. I am sure Mr. Miller would not object."

Sarah was pleased with Grace's small stitches, all carefully sewn. By sunset, the ladies completed James' and Micah's shifts; by bedtime, Benjamin's and Ethan's garments were completed as well.

The short days and long nights of winter followed a pattern. The men and boys worked in the woods from sunup to sunset, then Benjamin and Ethan studied their lessons in the evenings as James and Micah cared for the livestock and completed other necessary chores. No one had difficulties falling fast asleep at night. Each day Sarah would expand Grace's domestic horizons.

One morning Sarah announced, "Ethan needs a new great coat. I fear last winter I was negligent in my sewing and this winter that poor child's coat is worn and frayed."

"Are we going to make Ethan a new coat?"

"No, dear, not Ethan." Sarah teased.

"But you said –"

"We shall make Mr. Miller a new great coat. He shall pass his coat to Micah. They are now practically the same size. Micah shall hand his coat down to Benjamin. We will need to make some alterations, for Benjamin proves to be a late bloomer. Mark my words, the coat will fit him perfectly next winter," she said knowingly.

"Benjamin's coat will fit Ethan just as it is," Grace observed. "I see. If we make Mr. Miller a new coat, the result is everyone gets a newer and better coat than the one he had."

"If I was making this by myself, it would take nine days of carding, thirteen days of spinning, three days of weaving and three days of cutting.[7] However, I have you to assist me. We will card together for a couple of days to get a head start. Then I shall begin to spin as you continue to card. When the entire brown fleece is carded, you shall begin to spin."

"You know that I have tried spinning and I did poorly," Grace contradicted.

"The quality of your work was just fine. You were merely slow. The only remedy for that is practice, practice and more practice," Sarah stated emphatically. "We shall both sew the coat. When that is completed we shall make a couple of sensible work dresses for you."

"What about the yellow fleece?"

"The yellow fleece is yours to do as you wish. Upon completion of the coat and dresses you may spin and weave and make whatever you like."

"Well, let us begin!"

By late February everyone had a newer great coat and Grace had her "farm dresses."

"Ethan, could you teach me to make a basket?" Grace asked one evening.

"I would be more than happy to," he eagerly responded. He was flattered by her request, for no other member of his family, save for Abigail, had ever expressed a desire to learn the ancient craft. "I am half way through making this one. I could show you how to finish it for yourself, if you would like."

"Well yes, Ethan, I suppose I could learn how to end one before I begin one, but is that not rather opposite to the usual method? You know, I always thought one began a thing before one finished it."

"Oh, no, Grace, we must finish making all the weavers, all the ribs, and all the ovals before we attempt to begin the actual basket itself. Here, take this half basket and this weaver, have a seat right here."

The traditional egg basket that Ethan had begun earlier had its god's eyes completed on both ends of the stout, circular handle. They held in place a second ring perpendicular to the handle ring. This ring formed the top edge of the egg basket. Ethan had then filled one-half of the space formed by the two intersecting rings with a number of ribs that were evenly spaced so that about one-half of an inch of space separated the ribs at the widest point in the basket, whereas they touched each other at their ends – where the two rings as well as all the ends of the ribs were held together firmly by the decorative god's-eyes.

Ethan took great care to form the god's eyes with special weavers that were carefully split to be extremely thin yet especially long. Only when he had created a well-balanced pair of god's eyes on his basket did he proceed to finish it. The basket that he was now assigning to Grace had already been formed to shape and secured by a beautiful pair of large, yet graceful god's eyes that seemed to be too fine and graceful for such a humble egg basket. He had already added the first weavers on each side, next to the god's-eyes, and was about to add another row, when Grace took over. In truth, he was much more than half-finished with it.

Following Ethan's patient encouragements, Grace proceeded to add several more weavers, tuck the ends under where she could, and cut off the straggling ends where she could not hide them. When she was finished with her first basket, Grace sat for several minutes looking intently at her handiwork. [8]

About one inch from the top, Grace seamlessly wove a blue silk ribbon and tied a bow. "You ruined my basket!" Ethan complained. "No self-respecting farmer would be caught dead taking that thing into his barn!"

James gave his youngest son a warning glance.

"No, Ethan, I did not ruin *your* basket. I decorated *my* basket," she contradicted. "Cannot a basket be functional and yet beautiful as well? Perhaps a farmer would not appreciate such work, but I am certain his wife would proudly store her sewing or knitting in it. Perhaps she might buy one, if she saw it for sale at Mr. Frye's store."

"Miss Peabody, I admire your ingenuity," James complimented. "Ethan, please share some of your split ash and pine roots with Grace. And Grace, I will take you to Mr. Frye's store the next time I have a need to go. If he agrees to display them for sale, and as long as your other daily chores are completed, you may invest your free time pursuing your new business venture."

"Do you mean she will keep the money?" asked an incredulous Ethan. "What about me? I spent hours searching for and chopping down the ash tree, pounding the log to loosen the rings, making hundreds of weavers out of each one, steaming, bending, weaving, and teaching."

"Ethan, I shall purchase my supplies from you. I will give you a percentage of my profits," she shrewdly offered.

"We shall become business partners and equally share the profits," he countered. "Unless you would prefer chopping down your own trees and..."

"Benjamin, please draw up a business contract. Your brother and I are forming a business partnership."

"I would be delighted. Shall I bill you for my legal services?" he laughed.

"Would you be interested in bartering?"

"It depends upon what you are offering."

"I shall give you my father's copy of *Arabian Nights* in exchange for a business contract that will be legally binding in this household," she turned to James to judge whether he approved.

"Yes, the terms to which you and Ethan agree, will be binding in this household," James promised solemnly.

"Grace, I...I do not know what to say," Benjamin stammered. He never dreamed one day he would own such an expensive book.

"I believe 'thank you' would be appropriate on this occasion."

Micah stared at her in silent admiration. Not only was Grace Peabody beautiful and charming, she was brilliant, talented and industrious. He selfishly hoped that John Quincy Adams would never write her another letter and her father would never return to take her back to Boston.

At breakfast James asked, "What are you two industrious ladies planning to do today?"

"Mrs. Miller is going to teach me to weave on her loom."

"That is indeed a worthy endeavor."

"I am going to make a yellow apron and a yellow and brown plaid neckerchief to match my new work dresses."

"You are going to look like a bumble bee," Ethan teased.

"You mean the queen bee," Benjamin mumbled.

Grace laughed good-naturedly.

"Micah and I will be delivering a double-sled of firewood to Dr. Emery this morning. Sarah, please do not wait for us for dinner. We shall return by sunset."

"Benjamin and Ethan, I want you to spend the day stacking the firewood in the woodshed."

"Father, I am falling behind in my studies," Benjamin stated hoping to avoid another day of stacking wood.

"No, Benjamin, you are behind in your chores; your brother is behind in his studies. I have a proposal. The two of you will stack wood together until midmorning. Come in for tea and a geometry lesson until dinner. Is that agreeable to you, Benjamin?"

"Yes, Sir," he agreed amicably.

"After dinner, the two of you shall return to the wood-pile until midafternoon. Then you may return to continue your studies. Is there a novel that you would recommend for Ethan to read?"

"I believe he would enjoy *Gulliver's Travels*," Benjamin nodded.

"I do not wish for you to disturb the ladies' weaving today. You may light a fire in the drawing room and conduct your studies in there." James wisely understood that Benjamin would work more productively on the woodpile if he had a reward waiting for him at home.

A tranquil and productive day passed at Riverview Farm. Grace was delighted with her plaid fabric; Sarah was impressed with Grace's creativity. Benjamin was successful in teaching geometry in a manner which related to building furniture, staircases and slopes of roofs. He introduced Ethan to the 3-4-5 Right Triangle Rule and its many uses.

"As you know, whenever you have a triangle with a 90-degree angle, you refer to it as a Right Triangle. A triangle can only have one right angle. Also, there are only a total of 180 degrees in any triangle; therefore the other 2 angles combine to add up to the remaining 90 degrees."

"I remember this," Ethan nodded.

"However, you may not know: There is a combination of numbers that will always guarantee that you can find a true 90-degree angle anywhere you want to. For instance, Father used it at the corner of the house foundation to ensure that each granite block would be placed exactly at 90 degrees to define the house wall. He also used it to rack the bents before pegging them to be sure the posts were all parallel and straight and true to the frame. All summer, the carpenters were using it to square up interior wall layouts and such, as well as door frames and many other uses."

"Brother that is enough. Are you planning to let me in on this secret, or are you simply planning to talk me to death?"

"Ethan, it is simply stated thusly: whenever there is a right triangle whose two adjacent, or closest sides are 3 and 4, or any multiple of 3 and 4, then the hypotenuse, or long side, is always 5 or a multiple of 5. Therefore, when a right triangle has the shortest side of 3, and the next longest side is 4, then the third side is always 5.[9] See, here I have drawn it out for you on my slate:

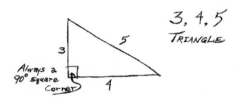

We can take the numbers 3,4 and 5 and do anything to them—add a number, multiply by a number, divide, change the lengths from inches to feet, fathoms, miles, whatever we want to do, and we can always be sure that the rule will hold. See here?

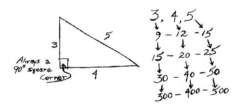

Whenever there is a 90-degree angle, we can find the hypotenuse of the triangle by using the 3-4-5 rule. Now, we can also check our carpenter's squares to be sure that they have a true 90-degree corner by simply measuring each leg of the square. Measuring 9 inches along the short side and measuring 12 inches along the long side, then measuring from each of these points to each other..."

"Yes! I can see now! Measuring between these points should be exactly 15 inches by the 3-4-5 rule!" shouted an excited Ethan. "This is amazing! Why could I not realize this before now? I often spied the carpenters with their marked lines measuring along the edges of the foundation, and then measuring a diagonal line, or measuring the diagonals of cabinet doors, or measuring diagonally across the space between two adjoining walls, and now I see why. It was not to measure the evenness of the edges, but to measure the squareness of the panels and the correctness of the wall angle—to find a true square corner. This is truly amazing!"

It was after sunset when the four of them sat down for their evening meal. "Perhaps Father and Micah are enjoying a meal with the Dr. and Mrs. Emery." Sarah tried to sound cheerful. "Will you two be making any baskets this evening?"

"No, Ma'am. I hope to read a few more chapters before going to bed," Ethan explained.

"I will begin sewing my new apron. I hope to-" Grace never finished her thought.

Micah came sprinting through the front door tracking mud into the foyer.

"Mercy, Micah!" Sarah chastised as she left the table and scurried into the foyer where Micah stood panting and gasping for breath.

"Did you run all the way home?" Benjamin asked in disbelief.

Micah's face was ashen; his body was trembling. "Mother, I am so sorry, so very sorry. There has been a terrible accident."

XII

Working Together

"**M**icah, come sit by the fire and tell us what happened," Sarah, struggling to remain calm, led him to the Liberty Table.

Catching his breath, her son replied. "We were pulling into Dr. Emery's yard when the sled skidded on some ice and landed in the ditch. We jumped off fearing the sled with all the firewood would tip over, but it did not. Hercules and Zeus could not drag the sled out. Before we had to unload all the wood, pull the sled out, then reload all the wood back in, Father instructed me to get behind the sled and push while he stood in front of the oxen and pulled.

Just as the sled was pulled out and back onto the road, Father must have slipped on that same patch of ice. He fell under Hercules and his left leg was crushed. I have never seen such ...." Micah covered his face with his hands. "I am so sorry, Mother," he sobbed.

In a maternal display of affection, she held him in her arms. "Hush, now. Do not carry burdens that are not yours to bear, for the burden will be too great. I have blamed myself for your sister's death for months. Finally I had to accept the sovereignty of God. I shall never understand why Abigail had to die. You may never understand why this accident had to happen. Do not blame yourself, Micah. Your father would not wish for you to become so distraught."

"He may never walk again. He may lose his leg. He may die!" he nervously ran his fingers through his hair.

"We shall not worry about what may happen. We will deal with what is before us now."

There was a pounding on the front door and Caleb Swan entered. "Mrs. Miller, I have just heard the news. How may I be of assistance?"

"Thank you, sir. You may take me to my husband now, please, and help Micah return the sled and oxen tomorrow morning, Mr. Swan." She disappeared into the pantry where she packed a large portion of dried comfrey, also called knit bone, into some clean linen strips. She would make several poultices and place them over the crushed bones[1]

Returning to the foyer she threw on her black, woolen cloak and instructed, "In your father's and my absence, Micah shall be the head of this house. You will respect and obey him as if he were your Father. Do I make myself understood, Benjamin?"

"Yes, Ma'am." Benjamin promised.

"Grace, you are perfectly capable of taking over the cooking and cleaning while I am gone. Mind your petticoats. My place is by my husband's side for as long as he needs me." With that, she hurried out the door with Caleb Swan by her side.

"I need to brush down the horses and check the livestock," Micah mumbled as he left for the barn. Benjamin found solace in reading books, Ethan in working with wood, and Micah in caring for his livestock. He brushed Aristotle and Socrates, his two prized possessions. He found comfort and meaning in being busy. Unlike Benjamin, he could not read for hours on end, ponder and brood about life. He needed to be outdoors, to be working, to be accomplishing something. He tried to keep down the terror in his heart. "What if Father dies? This farm, this family will be my responsibility." He wondered how Grace dealt with the uncertainty of her own father's fate.

When he returned to the kitchen he found a fine cooked meal of fried sausage, cornbread and chamomile tea on the table and Grace, Benjamin and Ethan sitting quietly.

"I fear that I shall never be able to fill Father's shoes," Micah confessed.

"Perhaps not by yourself, but by working together we will be able to fulfill all the responsibilities," Benjamin offered.

"Be ye strong and of good courage; be not afraid, neither be thou dismayed; for the LORD thy God is with thee whithersoever you go," Grace quoted Joshua 1:9.

Ethan and Benjamin looked at her incredulously. "I must tell you, I am not a total heathen." she returned their glares. "I listened to Reverend Fessenden's sermon on Sunday too, you know."

"Thank you for the meal, Grace. It has been an exhausting day and I think I will retire early. Ethan and Benjamin you may read until your accustomed bed time. Grace, will you be alright alone down here tonight?"

Grace indeed felt frightened, "If you would be kind enough to lock the doors, I shall be just fine," she smiled bravely.

At midnight, Grace heard the approach of horse and wagon and a forceful knocking on the front door. Peering through the front window she saw Reverend and Mrs. Fessenden standing in the moonlight and opened the door.

"Grace, we have come to..."

"No! No! He's dead! He's dead!" she shrieked. "Why do I lose everyone I love?" she sobbed uncontrollably.

The brothers ran downstairs barefoot wearing their new linen shifts. Only Micah had taken the time to put on his britches.

"Father is dead?" Ethan's lower lip quivered.

"No! No! My goodness, no one is dead," Reverend Fessenden explained. "What I tried to say at the door was that we have come to spend the night, for your mother was concerned it was not proper leaving the four of you alone." He glanced at the young men who were in various stages of undress. Grace was modestly draped in a lavender silk dressing gown.

"I shall make us tea, Grace offered." We are all now very wide awake and I fear no one shall sleep much tonight."

The brothers returned to the table properly attired. "Let us pray for your father's recovery," the good Reverend offered.

Benjamin had not prayed since the day his sister died. Had he not prayed faithfully and fervently for his sister's recovery? Had he not trusted God with all his heart? Yet, Abigail died anyway. Clearly, God was not worthy of his trust, never mind his devotion and adoration.

The minister wisely read the skepticism in Benjamin's eyes. "Everyone dies. Some die at an early age in their mothers' arms. Others live a long and prosperous life and die surrounded by their children and grandchildren. Some die gallantly on the battlefield; others die suddenly in a senseless act of violence. Yet no one ever dies alone because the Lord is always with them.

Your father does not fear death, for his trust is in his Lord and Savior. His only concern is for his family. And little Abigail knew when she was dying. She also did not fear, for she knew she would only be restored to full health in the next world. Everyone dies. It is only a question of when.

We do not and we should not pray that the Lord answers our prayers the way we wish Him to. We will pray that He will give us the courage to accept that His will, regardless of how painfully we may personally find it to be, is for the best. We are not the masters who expect God to serve us. But we are the servants of our Lord and Heavenly Father."

That night Micah, Benjamin, Ethan and Grace understood with certainty that there was Someone greater than they. And they all knew that Someone was in control.

The next morning Grace made hasty pudding without mishap. "This is good, Grace," Ethan complimented with his mouth full. "I had feared that I would starve in mother's absence."

"That is good to know," Sarah smiled. Mr. Swan had taken her home when he returned the sled and oxen.

"How is Father?" the brothers asked anxiously.

Sarah sat down wearily. "He is in much pain. He cannot be moved and will stay at Dr. Emery's for several weeks, perhaps months. I pray that no infection will set in. We must take one day at a time. I shall take a brief rest before I return to your father. Micah, please pick me up at Dr. Emery's this evening before you retire. Ethan, I have a message from Father," she smiled. "The sap is running."

"I will gather the buckets. Are you coming, Grace?" Ethan invited.

"I am sorry but I have my morning chores—gathering the eggs, feeding the sheep, making dinner, weaving." She saw Ethan's disappointment. "Do you want your dinner? Then I must stay home. However, I will go out this afternoon. There is an ash tree I wish to inspect more closely."

The wagon was almost loaded by the time Grace appeared in the barn with her egg basket. "Have you ever gathered the eggs by yourself? The rooster can be rather ornery," Micah warned.

"Samuel Adams does not frighten me."

"Samuel Adams? Grace, what are you talking about?" Benjamin asked in exasperation.

"I named the rooster Samuel Adams because all he does all day is strut about and squawk." Micah's laughter filled the barn. "Ouch! You are an incorrigible creature!" she addressed the rooster after he pecked her right hand. "If you do that again, you will end up in the stew pot!"

At noon, when the boys returned hungry; their dinner was plentiful. Grace threw on Ethan's discarded great coat, climbed into the wagon by Micah's side and enjoyed an afternoon of fresh air and the strenuous labor of emptying sap buckets into the collection barrels. That evening, the boys set up the large iron pot outdoors over a fire and began the long process of boiling down maple sap into maple sugar. Grace, meanwhile, continued her weaving. Before bedtime, Micah returned home with his exhausted mother.

"There is no fever, no infection. We will continue to take one day at a time."

That was the daily routine the family followed for the next two weeks of that spring. Sarah would spend the day with James; Micah would bring her home in the evening. On Sundays they attended church and briefly visited James who was very weak and in pain. One Monday morning, Micah was clearly anxious as he ran his fingers nervously through his hair. He skipped breakfast and said, "I am going to Mr. Frye's store to see if I can sell the horses."

Micah knew that farm animals were not pets or members of the family; they were a business investment, a mode of transportation, a source of income or one's next meal. However, he raised Socrates and Aristotle from foals; they were his pride and joy.

"Why?" gasped Grace.

"It has been several weeks since Father's accident. We now owe Dr. Emery a substantial debt. Father is just being practical. The horses will bring a good price and we still have the oxen for transportation."

"I guess we ran out of Grace's petticoats," Ethan said sadly.

Grabbing her fur lined, indigo wool cloak she declared," I am going with you to see if Ethan and I have sold any baskets." They rode together in silence. Micah brooded about the horses, while Grace was lost in her own thoughts.

"Young lady, I am delighted to see you this morning," Mr. Frye greeted Grace. "I sold all six of your baskets and I would like to order ten more."

"I must tell you, I am surprised they all sold so quickly."

"Well, you know how news travels quickly in Fryeburg. Mr. Swan bought one for his wife and then Mrs. Walker wanted one just like it. Of course, when Mrs. Knight saw it, she bought two for herself. Mrs. Dresser bought one for her daughter and one for Mrs. Fessenden. My wife wants an extra-large one and Mrs. Evans would like one with a pink ribbon. This week they are flying out the door."

"Sir," Micah began nervously, "my father wishes to sell our horses. He would like to know if you or if someone you know would be interested."

"First, Mr. Frye, I am interested in selling my cloak. It is imported from London and is more valuable than four horses! Besides, how many horses are there already in Fryeburg? There is only one cloak like this one. Because we currently find ourselves in financially precarious circumstances, I will sacrifice this cloak for the price of three horses."

"You are quite the business woman, Miss Peabody," Joseph Frye laughed. "It is a deal."

"Grace, you cannot do that," Micah objected.

"Sir, I just did."

"I will not allow it."

"Micah Bradford Miller you are neither my father nor my husband. Even if you were, I still would not listen."

"But, I promised Father that I would sell the horses."

"You may sell them to me, then. I have plenty of money now," she smiled brightly at Mr. Frye who was handing her a leather pouch of coins.

On the way home, Micah glanced at her shyly and said," I do not know how to ever thank you."

"A simple 'thank you' shall suffice." came her quiet answer.

"Why did you do it? You loved that cloak."

"You loved those horses more. Next fall I shall make myself a new cloak. I will card the fleece, spin it, weave it and sew it myself."

"I will go trapping next winter myself, and then you can line it with pure ermine fur," he promised .He looked directly into her eyes and added, "Thank you, Grace. Thank you."

The snow melted with the passing of time, the mud eventually disappeared, the forsythias bloomed; it was spring in the Saco River Valley. The danger of frost had passed; it was now time to plow the fields and plant.

Grace found Micah in the barn grooming Socrates and Aristotle after breakfast. "I cannot do this," he confessed, running his fingers through his hair. "We barely had enough firewood and food this winter – that was with Father and I and a few hired hands working."

"Ethan and Benjamin will help."

"Do not think me ungrateful for my brothers, but farming is a man's job. The two of them are no substitute for Father. Please ask Ethan to come out and hitch Hercules and Zeus to the plow. Ask Benjamin to draw the water, feed the livestock, bring in the day's firewood and continue stacking the firewood in the shed. Do not wait for me for dinner. I wish to plow all day without interruption."

When Micah and Ethan were safely out of view, Grace turned to Benjamin who was bringing a bucket of water to the hearth. "This is for you," he grinned first to the fire in the hearth and then to her hemline.

She ignored his comment. "Please bring me to the Fessenden's. I wish to speak to the good Reverend."

"What about?"

"The Lord's work," she replied mysteriously.

It was sunset when Micah and Ethan returned to the barn, unhitched the oxen and wearily entered the kitchen.

"Grace, what did you do?" Micah pointed to her right hand neatly wrapped with a clean linen bandage.

"Do not be concerned. After I was able to stop the bleeding, I made an infusion of Chamomile, soaked a bandage in it, and applied the compress to my wounds. I shall be fine."[2]

"I am famished!" Ethan declared as he sat down at the table. "What smells so good?"

Grace smiled wickedly, "Rooster stew."

Caleb Swan entered the barn the next morning. "I have come to help with the planting today."

"Well, th-thank you, Sir," Micah stammered in surprise. "What about your own farm?"

"It will still be there tomorrow," he smiled. "I think I can spare one day to help my closet friend." Micah was not only grateful for this generous man's labor, but for his encouragement as well.

Early the next morning, there was a knock at the kitchen door. "Mr. Benjamin, am I too late for breakfast?"

"Limbo, my friend, come on in," Benjamin greeted as he pointed to an empty chair. "Please have a seat and join us. I am afraid it will be a very short reading lesson today. I must help with the planting."

"I am not here to see you, Mr. Benjamin. I am here to help Mr. Micah with the plowing. Mr. Osgood sent me today. He said if the tables were turned your father would have helped us."

"Something is wrong!" Micah sat straight up in his bed in the middle of the night. He looked around the expansive second floor and could see his brothers asleep in their beds. He felt uneasy. Suddenly he heard the sheep and the horses braying frantically. Looking out his window he saw a large catamount in the dim moonlight circling the barn.

He threw on his britches, ran down the back stairs, and grabbed his father's musket above the mantel. His hands shook as he loaded the gun and quietly walked out the back door with his eyes glued to the barn. Micah understood his first shot must prove fatal for there is nothing more dangerous than a wounded wild animal. He saw two green eyes glowing in the darkness at the corner of the barn. He aimed and pulled the trigger. The large cat silently fled across the fields and into the woods. Although he had missed, the gun shot produced the desired effect, for it was gone.

His brothers, his mother and Grace ran out the back door shouting, "What is it?"

"Everything is fine. Go back to bed," Micah instructed.

"What is going on?" Grace demanded.

"It was a catamount. But I frightened him away."

"What happens if it returns?" Ethan asked.

"We should build a fire between the house and the barn. That may persuade it to not return," Benjamin suggested. "That is what Father would do."

Ethan, secretly relieved when Benjamin volunteered to keep watch with Micah, returned to the house with Grace and Sarah. At sunrise, they discovered the cat's tracks around the barn and a spot where it had tried to dig under the barn door. After breakfast Micah took Sarah to her daily visit to Dr. Emery's to stay with James.

Upon Micah's return, Abraham Bradley appeared on horseback with a loaded rifle. "Good morning," he tipped his hat. "I see you also had a visitor last night."

"Was it at your place too?" Micah attempted to sound nonchalant in front of his younger brothers.

"I followed its tracks from my barn to here to up that mountain," he nodded to the west. "Do you care to join me?"

Micah swallowed hard before replying. "Yes, sir."

"Micah, this is not like going deer hunting. This is dangerous," Benjamin warned.

"A man needs to protect his family and property," Micah countered.

"What would your mother say?" Grace challenged.

"She would say, 'Be careful, Micah'." He smiled. "Ethan and Benjamin, you tend to the livestock then return immediately to the house. There will be no planting today. The three of you are to stay indoors. Grace and Ethan you can spend the day weaving baskets. And you," he turned to Benjamin, "may read and review Ethan's geometry."

Micah and Mr. Bradley hiked for hours before tracking the catamount up the mountain. When they finally found it, the creature was watching them from above, perched high in a tree. Micah took aim and fired. The wounded animal shrieked as it leapt from its perch. A shot rang out from Mr. Bradley's rifle and the cat fell dead at his feet.[3]

The next morning, Joseph Frye's two rugged sons, Joseph and Nathaniel, greeted Micah in the barn. "Father heard you were occupied yesterday and you might be a day behind in your plowing," the elder brother grinned. Both sons had recently returned home from the War.

"News sure travels fast in Fryeburg," Micah shook his head.

"What?" Nathaniel asked.

"I said 'News travels fast!'" he yelled. Nathaniel Frye had lost his hearing while fighting in the Battle of Monmouth in New Jersey[4]. He nodded in agreement and smiled.

That evening Micah was an exhausted but thankful young man; the plowing and planting was finally done. Reverend Fessenden brought Sarah home that evening. "Your father shall be returning home tomorrow," she smiled.

If the boys were expecting life to return to "normal" upon their father's arrival, they were sadly mistaken. James could barely walk even short distances with the aid of a cane and his wife.

"It is good to be home," the gaunt, exhausted James said as he entered the foyer and looked around. "I hear that my family has made me proud."

"James, I believe a celebration is in order. Let us take a seat in the drawing room. Ethan, please grab a stool, Benjamin please bring pillows from my bed. Micah, please help me get your father comfortable. Grace, please make us some tea—I believe your best china would well serve the occasion."

"What I really would like, Grace is a big bowl of rooster stew," James winked.

"Sir, I must tell you, he had it coming!"

Each morning from planting through harvest, a volunteer would arrive to help with the day's farm work. With the end of the War and the return of the veterans, there was no shortage of extra manpower. Certain young men volunteered on numerous occasions. Micah was certain it was not altruism, but Grace's charm that drew them for return visits. Some of the older men, visited with James in the afternoon after working a few hours in the morning.

James, who did not have the strength to walk the acres of his fields, inspected his crops on horseback. He often grew impatient and frustrated and feared he would never be able to do a man's work again.

"Things will be different next year," Sarah often reassured her husband.

Crops were not the only things growing. Benjamin and Grace matured into adulthood. To Grace's dismay, most of her wardrobe which she brought from Boston two years earlier were impossibly snug. She now began wearing her mother's open gowns and petticoats to church. Micah had to share his meager outfits with his tall and lanky younger brother.

One November evening, Grace abruptly stopped weaving the wool cloth designated to become her new winter cloak. She spread out her old blue silk petticoat on the Liberty Table and began cutting and sewing. Two days later she had made two men's silk shifts, one for Benjamin and one for Micah.

"Benjamin, your mother and I decided that an attorney should not appear in court dressed like a farmer. This will look rather attractive with the black waistcoat and frock coat which we shall make later this year.

"I do not believe a farmer should look like an attorney. Perhaps I should have both of them," Benjamin teased.

"You most certainly will not. I intend to keep this for a special occasion, like a wedding, perhaps," Micah smiled at a blushing Grace. The War had ended eleven months ago with no sign of Mr. William Peabody's return. Grace no longer talked of her Papa coming home.

The winter passed quickly for Grace. She now spent her days spinning, weaving, designing and making clothing for the family from interesting combinations of new cloth and remnants of her old outfits. She was designing and sewing a patchwork quilt of exquisite, silk fabrics sewed on a striking, black wool background. Many evenings were devoted to writing letters to her grandparents and many cousins whom she had never met.

She enjoyed her third maple syrup season as much as her first. Now, of course, she no longer needed Ethan to point out which trees were maple trees.

The following summer, James bravely attempted to do as much farm work his limp and cane would allow. He sadly realized that he would no longer be able to plow the fields that he loved. Fortunately, nineteen-year-old Micah was a strong and rugged man; sixteen-year-old Benjamin and fourteen-year-old Ethan contributed valuable labor.

James and Benjamin had come to a mutual understanding. Benjamin would pack his books away from June through October and unselfishly devote his labors to the farm. In return, he could retire to the quiet, contemplative life of a scholar from November to May.

Sarah eagerly received a letter from her beloved friend, Abigail.

Braintree, Massachusetts
October, 1783

My Dearest Sarah,

I have just received a letter from John in Paris and I had to write you. On September 3, 1783, John, Benjamin Franklin and John Jay signed the treaty in Paris[4] that officially draws the War to a close..."

Eight years after the Battle at Lexington and Concord, and seven years after the Declaration of Independence the American Colonies were now officially a new nation.[5]

"I must tell you. This is call for a celebration. I shall make us a pot of tea."

XIII

The Reunion

I t was a glorious spring afternoon in May of 1784 when James sat peacefully in the drawing room reading his Bible. He had slowly come to accept his limitations; over-exertion this morning resulted in spending many hours with his injured leg propped up on pillows. Micah and Ethan were out in the barn; Benjamin had just left in the wagon to pick up Sarah and Grace who were sewing with some ladies at Mrs. Knight's home.

He was startled by a knocking on the front door. Aided by his hickory cane carved by Ethan, he limped to the door and found a thin, elegantly dressed, elderly man with an ivory tipped, mahogany cane anxiously surveying the grounds.

"Good day, sir," James warmly greeted. "How may I be of assistance?"

"I am told this is the home of James and Sarah Miller. My name is Edward Smyth and I am, I was," he corrected, "the first mate on *The Sweet Elizabeth*. I understand Miss Grace Alden Peabody now resides with you."

"Yes, sir, Grace has lived with us now for over three years—since her mother died. Please, do come in," he invited.

The distinguished guest glanced around the foyer and large staircase before entering the drawing room. "I see that Grace managed to bring her furniture from home."

"She brought more than furniture," James laughed. He retold the story of the golden petticoats. My sons and I had a frame and lumber prepared to build a barn. However, we ended up building this luxurious addition to our modest home instead."

"I believe she made a wise investment," he nodded. "I am here to see Grace."

"She and my wife are visiting and will return shortly. Please have a seat and make yourself comfortable while you await her arrival."

"Is the child well? Is she in good health? Is she in good spirits?" he inquired.

James laughed. "I understand her father called her The Amazing Grace. Truly there is no other name better suited." Like a proud father he regaled stories of her arrival, her adventures and her mishaps.

"I see she has found a loving home here."

"Father?" Micah and Ethan entered the room.

"Mr. Smyth, may I present to you my two sons, Micah and Ethan Miller. Sons, this is Mr. Edward Smyth, first mate on Mr. Peabody's ship. He has stopped in to visit with Grace."

Micah eyed him suspiciously, for this gentleman appeared to be too old and too wealthy to be a first mate.

Benjamin stopped the wagon at the front door to help the ladies down before continuing to the barn. Glancing through the front window, Mr. Smyth gasped, "She is no longer a child! She has grown to be a beautiful woman like her mother."

Micah greeted the women in the foyer. "Grace, you have a visitor waiting to see you in the drawing room."

She hurriedly entered the room, stopped and silently stared at the guest.

He slowly took a few steps toward her and outstretched his arms. "I promised you I would return," he spoke gently.

"Papa?" she whispered in disbelief. "Papa! Mama told me you were alive. I stopped hoping... Papa, is it really you?"

"Yes, my Amazing Grace, it is I. I never stopped searching for you since my release last September." Father and daughter wept openly as they embraced.

"Sir, I do not understand," Micah stated in bewilderment.

"I am afraid it is a very long story," William Peabody smiled.

"Papa, we have plenty of time to listen. Of course, you shall stay with us."

"I shall be delighted to accept your hospitality before returning to Boston."

The evening meal was served in the dining room, on the Peabody's mahogany table, covered with the linens and served on china Grace brought from Boston. Gazing at Elizabeth's portrait hung over the mantel, William sighed, "I feel right at home, here. How your mother begged me not to leave that morning! Oh, how I regret not heeding her pleas.

During one of my many visits to Philadelphia, I happened to make my acquaintance with John Adams. I had always wanted to meet the man after I watched him defend his client - the British officer involved in the Boston Massacre. Therefore, I was delighted when he accepted my offer to join me for a late supper. It was after that meal when he asked me if I was willing to volunteer my considerable smuggling talents on behalf of the Patriots. How I do despise that term. We Peabodys prefer 'discreet importing'.

Mr. Adams explained that with no means for producing arms and gunpowder, the colonies were dependent on clandestine shipments from Europe.[1] His arguments were so compelling; I felt I had no recourse but to oblige. I thought since I was sailing to Europe to pick up tea in Amsterdam, it would be only a minor inconvenience to conceal the contraband amongst the tea. I do hate to boast, but I was extremely successful in these endeavors. One day *The Sweet Elizabeth* docked with 49,000 pounds of gun powder.[2]

Of course I could not reveal my activities to you, Grace or to your mother. Because I feared for my family's safety if I should ever be captured, I sailed under the identity of a fictional First Mate-Edward Smyth. In this manner, if there was an incident in which I was unable to return home, a message could be sent informing her to the whereabouts of Mr. Smyth."

"That is why Mama insisted that you were still alive and everyone else was wrong. Mama knew the truth all along." Grace now realized her mother's dilemma of reassuring her child that her Papa was still alive, yet without betraying her husband's secret.

Unfortunately, the British ambushed us in Delaware Bay a few miles out from Philadelphia. The explosion blew me off the deck. I swam away from the inferno into the arms of my captors who held me in the hold of their ship for months before sailing to London. There was no way I could send word to my family. I was not released until the Paris Peace Treaty was signed."

"That is why you did not return at the end of the war—I mean after the Battle of York Town—like many of our local veterans." Grace now understood the situation.

"I took the first vessel headed to America; it landed in Philadelphia. My friends there convinced me to stay with them to rest and to regain my health before beginning my journey to Boston. I wrote several letters to your mother, but never received a reply. After weeks of recuperation, I finally headed for home.

Imagine my dismay when, upon my arrival in Boston I learned that both my parents and wife had died. I found my cousin Thomas and his family living in my house. I also discovered that Thomas had sold and auctioned my parents' home and belongings and kept the proceeds for himself. But the worst of it all was no one knew where you were. I traveled to Braintree hoping to find you living with Mrs. Abigail Adams. She and her daughter Nabby had just left for Paris to be with Mr. Adams.[3] I traveled to Weymouth hoping that Mr. and Mrs. Smith, Abigail's parents, may have known of your whereabouts. Unfortunately, both were deceased. In desperation I went to visit the Bradford's, who informed me that Grace was living with their daughter, Sarah Bradford Miller in Fryeburg in the Province of Maine.

And here I find my little girl has matured into a beautiful young woman."

Micah sat silently distraught. What were this man's intentions? Did he presume after all these years, he would return to Boston with Grace?

"Mr. Peabody, after our meal may I escort you on a short tour of our farm?" James invited.

During their walk, William Peabody confessed, "Mr. Miller I simply do not know how to repay you and your family for your kindness to my daughter. I intend to sell *The Amazing Grace*, give you the proceeds, divest myself of my partnership in the business and retire comfortably in Boston with my daughter."

"Mr. Peabody, your generosity is admirable. However, you have already provided us with the means to build this home. We have more than everything we need. Grace was never a burden to us; indeed, she has become a member of our family."

"Mr. Miller, if you do not want money, could I buy more farm land for your sons' future perhaps? It is a father's responsibility to establish their sons in a trade."

"Well, sir, there is one thing…"

Three days later Mr. Peabody approached his daughter, "Are you ready to return to Boston with me? I shall need your assistance in selecting and decorating our new home."

"Sir, my home is here now", she stated firmly. "We shall endeavor to visit you often, but I choose to remain here."

"Young lady, you give me no choice. I fear I must return to Boston alone, attend to my business affairs, and then retire at Riverview Farm," he threatened jovially.

Micah sighed with relief as Grace clapped her hands in delight. "Now my family is complete."

"I do not feel it wise for an old man like myself to make this trip alone again" continued the visitor. That is why I insist on taking Benjamin with me. We shall travel together - all the way to Harvard College."

"I do not understand," Benjamin looked to his father, then to his mother.

"Son, Mr. Peabody has generously offered to pay your expenses to study law at Harvard," Sarah explained.

"Mother,"

"You must go, Benjamin. Abigail Adams is not the only mother with a brilliant son," She laughed.

After the plowing and planting was completed, but long before harvest, Benjamin James Miller loaded three heavy trunks onto the back of a wagon – two filled with books and one with clothing. He could not conceal his tears as he bid his family farewell. He gave his mother one last hug.

"Mr. Benjamin! Mr. Benjamin!" Limbo came running up the lane.

"Limbo, my friend!" he shook the African's hand.

"Mr. Osgood gave me my own quill, ink pot and parchment. I will write you letters."

"And I shall write you back."

The Millers, Grace and Limbo stood in the dooryard watching the wagon slowly leave Fryeburg and head toward Benjamin's future.

Discussion Questions

1. Political turmoil and battles do not merely affect politicians and soldiers; they impact civilians and families. These events do not impact all families equally. What impact did having the husband/father leave the family to serve his country have on the family? How did the following events affect the fictional Miller family, the fictional Peabody family and the historical Adams family?

   A. The Boston Massacre
   B. The Quartering Act
   C. The Townsend Act
   D. The Boston Tea Party
   E. The Battle of Lexington and Concord
   F. Washington's attack on Boston
   G. The Declaration of Independence
   H. Supplying the Colonies with gunpowder

2. Compare and contrast the economy of Fryeburg, Maine during the Revolutionary War to today's global economy. What is the role of manufacturing? What is the role of bartering? What is the role of the father, mother and children in meeting the family's needs?

3. Compare and contrast the socio/economic environment of Fryeburg and Boston during the Revolutionary War. In what town would you have preferred to live? Why?

4. Discuss the gender roles as portrayed in the Miller, Peabody and Adams families.

5. List the accomplishments and education of the teenage Miller brothers. How do these compare to those of teenagers today?

6. What did James mean when he told Limbo that "the ground in front of the cross is perfectly level"? Find Scripture to corroborate this belief. Were James' actions consistent with his beliefs? Explain.

7. List the many crafts and skills portrayed in this novel. Select one or two activities which you or your family would like to learn and work on a project.

8. Visit your local historical society and library to learn about the history of your town.

End Notes

Chapter I The Loss

1. The Fryeburg Village Cemetery was established in 1786. The author here took a literary license.
2. John S. Barrows, <u>Fryeburg Maine An Historical Sketch</u> (Fryeburg, ME: Pequawket Press, 1938), p. 29-30.
3. Nancy Ondra, <u>The A-Z Guide to Herbs that Heal</u> (Emmaus, PA: Rodale Press, 1995)
4. Debra Friedman and Jack Larkin, editors, <u>Old Sturbridge Village Cookbook</u> (Guilford, CT: Three Forks, 2009), p. 113 *"Indian Pudding Recipe"*.

Chapter II The Letters

1. David McCullough, <u>John Adams</u> (New York: Simon & Schuster, 2001), p. 59.
2. McCullough p. 61.
3. McCullough p. 62
4. Henry F. Graff, Editor, <u>The Presidents A Reference History – 2nd Edition</u>. (New York: Simon & Schuster Macmillan, 1997), p. 92.
5. McCullough p.63.

6. McCullough p.65-66.
7. McCullough p. 66.
8. McCullough p. 66-68
9. McCullough p. 66.
10. Barrows p. 7.
11. McCullough p. 69.
12. Ibid.
13. http://en.wikipedia.org/wiki/Townshend_Acts
14. http://en.wikipedia.org/wiki/Boston_Tea_Party
15. Ibid. 11.
16. McCullough p. 22.
17. http://en.wikipedia.org/wiki/The Battle of Lexington and Concord
18. McCullough p. 72-74.
19. McCullough p. 75.
20. McCullough p. 76.
21. The Complete Idiot's Guide to the American Revolution p. 154.
22. McCullough p. 76.
23. McCullough p. 77

Chapter III More Letters

1. http://www.NelMA.org. "The King's Broad Arrow and Eastern White Pine" (ac. 9/2010)
2. McCullough p. 171.
3. McCullough p. 172.
4. McCullough p. 176.

Chapter IV The Geometry Lesson

1. McCullough p. 243-244.
2. Using the Pythagorean Theorem to calculate the length of a rafter described by Wayne O'Donal.
3. Graphics drawn by Wayne O'Donal

Chapter V The Arrival

1. A lifetime of observations in the woods by Wayne O'Donal
2. http://en.wikipedia.org/wiki/ThomasChippendale
3. Bobbie Kalman, 18<u>th</u> <u>Century Clothing</u> (New York: Crabtree Publishing Company, 1993), p. 10-18
4. Barrows p. 241-242

Chapter VI The Lord's Day

1. <u>http://www.oldnorth.com/HistoryandArchitecture.</u> <u>htm</u> accessed 10/2010
2. Barrows p. 83-84
3. <u>http://www.accessgeneology.com/maine/fryeburg.</u> <u>htm</u> accessed 10/2010
4. Barrows p. 36-37.
5. Barrows p. 51-59
6. Barrows p. 94, 97
7. Barrows p. 51-59
8. <u>http://www.plantcultures.org/plants/indigohistory.</u> <u>htm</u> accessed 10/201
9. "Hearthside Recipes" Remick Country Doctor Museum and Farm Hearthside Dinner, January 22, 2011

Chapter VII The Promise of Spring

1. Barrows p. 13-14
2. Description of a spice box as seen at the Freeman's Farm House in Old Sturbridge Village in Sturbridge, MA 2/21/11
3. Kalman p. 13

Chapter VIII The Raising

1. The description of the hand-raising and division of labor by Wayne O'Donal

Chapter IX A Summer to Remember

1. C. Keith Wilbur, Home Building and Woodworking in Colonial America (Guilford, CT: Globe Pequot Press, 1992), p. 52
2. Wilbur p. 50
3. Wilbur p. 71
4. Wilbur p. 62
5. Wilbur p. 66
6. Ibid.
7. Wilbur p. 86
8. Wilbur p. 75
9. http.//www.woodcarversguild.com.htm. accessed 3/2011
10. Ibid.
11. Ibid.
12. Ibid.

Chapter X The Beauty of Autumn

1. Rita Buchanan, <u>A Dyer's Garden-From Plant to Pot-Growing Dyes for Natural Fibers</u>
2. (Loveland, CO: Interweave Press, 1999) "Goldenrod"
3. Ibid.
4. McCullough p. 262
5. Ibid

Chapter XI A Very Long Winter

1. Paul Johnson, <u>A History of the American People</u> (New York: Harper Collins, 1998), p. 29
2. McCullough, p
3. Kalman, p. 4
4. Recipes from the "Sausage Making Workshop" Remick Country Doctor and Farm Museum, March, 2011.
5. Visit to The Old Sturbridge Village, Sturbridge, MA on February 2011
6. Meredith Wright, <u>Every Day Dress of Rural America 1783-1800</u> (New York: Dover Books, 1992), "Directions for Making a Shift"
7. Visit to the Exhibit "A Coat in Thirty Days" at The Old Sturbridge Village, in Sturbridge, MA on February 2011
8. Description of basket weaving by Wayne O'Donal

Chapter XII Working Together

1. Nancy Ondra, editor <u>The A-Z Guide to Herbs that Heal</u> (Emmaus, PA: Rodale Press, 1995), p.
2. Barrows p.

3. McCullough p. 285
4. Ibid.

Chapter XIII The Reunion

1. 1. McCullough p. 78
2. 2. McCullough p. 79

Bibliography

Barrows, John Stuart. Fryeburg Maine An Historical Sketch. Fryeburg, ME. Pequawket Press. 1938.

Buchanan, Rita. A Dyer's Garden – From Plant to Pot-Growing Dyes for Natural Fibers. Loveland, CO. Interweave Press. 1999

Friedman, Debra and Larkin, Jack, editors. Old Sturbridge Village Cookbook. Guilford, CT. Three Forks. 2009.

Graff, Henry F., editor. The Presidents A Reference History. New York. Simon & Schuster Macmillan. 1997

"Hearthside Recipes". Tamworth. NH. Remick Country Doctor Museum. Hearthside Dinner, January 22, 2011.

Johnson, Paul. A History of the America People. New York. Harper Collins. 1998

Kalman, Bobbie. 18th Century Clothing. New York. Crabtree Publishing Company. 1993

McCullough, David. John Adams. New York. Simon & Schuster. 2001

Ondra, Nancy, editor. The A-Z Guide to Herbs that Heal. Emmaus, PA. Rodale Press. 1995

Wilbur, C. Keith. Home Building and Woodworking in Colonial America. Guilford, CT. Globe Pequot Press. 1992

Wright, Meredith. <u>Every Day Dress of Rural America 1783-1800</u>. New York. Dover Books. 1992

http://www.NeLMA.org The King's Broad Arrow and Eastern White Pine.

http://www.plantcultures.org/plants/indigo_history.htm

http://www.woodcarversguild.com.htm

http:/www.accessgeneolgoy.com/maine/Fryeburg.htm.

About the Author and the Fryeburg Chronicles

A uthor, June O'Donal, is a nineteen year homeschooling veteran who is convinced that history is fascinating and relevant; textbooks are boring and irrelevant. She has read with her children countless autobiographies, biographies and historical fiction from ancient Egypt to present day. As the founding editor of "Brain Storm" Magazine and former member of the Board of Directors of the Maine Brain Injury Association, she discovered she enjoyed researching, writing and editing. As a 1977 graduate of Gordon College with a degree in sociology, she has continued to observe how the culture impacts the family and how the family unit impacts the culture.

The Amazing Grace is written for the casual novel reader as well as for the history buff. The discussion questions may be useful for book clubs, homeschoolers or school groups. The Fryeburg Chronicles will be a series of historical fiction following the lives of the Miller family and their descendants as they experience local and national events.

In The Fryeburg Chronicles Book II, Attorney Benjamin Miller returns to Fryeburg from Philadelphia in 1792 to become the first headmaster of a new school named Fryeburg Academy. Neither his family nor the town is aware of his secret and his promise. The Secret and the Promise is scheduled for the fall of 2012.

Additional copies of the Fryeburg Chronicles can be ordered through your local book store, from the following e-retailers, Amazon.com, Barnes & Noble and Google Books, or directly from the publisher www.XulonPress.com.

CPSIA information can be obtained at www.ICGtesting.com
Printed in the USA
269620BV00001B/2/P